Blood on the Reaper

B.J. HOLMES

A Black Horse Western

ROBERT HALE · LONDON

© B.J. Holmes 1992
First published in Great Britain 1992

ISBN 0 7090 4882 3

Robert Hale Limited
Clerkenwell House
Clerkenwell Green
London EC1R 0HT

For another Sarah

Photoset in North Wales by
Derek Doyle & Associates, Mold, Clwyd.
Printed in Great Britain by
St Edmundsbury Press Ltd, Bury St Edmunds, Suffolk.
Bound by WBC Bookbinders Ltd, Bridgend, Mid-Glamorgan.

BLOOD ON THE REAPER

Foreword

The continuing absence of law along the western
frontier of the United States during the latter half
of the last century led to the phenomenon known
to history as 'the bounty-hunter'. Unfortunately for
students of the period, no systematic contemporary
record was kept of the payment from public funds
made to private citizens for delivery to the
authorities of wanted persons. Therefore, as the
evidence of their very existence is anecdotal,
compounded by myth and legend, there can be no
quantitative comparisons, no grisly league tables.

However, study of a particularly valuable cache
of historical documents now lodged in the Archive
Department of the Calpone Foundation Library
has shown the name of one recipient of bounty
payments to appear with noticeable regularity
during the period. Nothing is known about him
apart from his name, Jonathan Grimm, and that
records show his fading signature on receipts for
twenty-six men brought in dead or alive. With the
data being incomplete, the actual figure that could
be credited to him is likely to be even greater.
Irrespective, the statistic as it stands must put him
at, or near, the top of the league table of those men

who earned their living by this questionable means.

The following text recounts an episode in that man's life. While there is no extant evidence as to its particulars, neither is there any to the contrary.

ONE

He heard the door creak to his side and he whirled round, one of his Army forty-fours ready to mete out bloody deserts to yet another hard-case. Just in time he stopped himself putting pressure on the hair-trigger.

In the doorway stood a young girl. She wore a brown cloth pelisse, cut plain and straight, hooked and eyed down the front, fastened at the waist with a cord. It was difficult to tell her age with any exactitude. The pelisse masked her figure and the features of her face were barely discernible deep in the shadow of a drab bonnet. But she was small, less than four feet; that alone indicated tender years.

'Pa!' she screamed, and ran past Grimm, dropping on to the fallen man, the man that the bounty-hunter had just despatched to hell and beyond with one clean shot through the heart.

'Judas Priest,' Grimm mouthed to himself. He couldn't remember the tally of no-goods he'd killed during his career, but this, shooting a man in front of his kid, this was a new marble to pull out of the bag. He breathed deep and tense as the bottom dropped out of his stomach. Sickened, he watched the girl pull at lifeless limbs, trying to hold up the slack head. When she saw the blood she made an animal noise and recoiled.

'You killed him! You killed Pa!' She turned, faced Grimm directly so that he could more easily make out the almost infant features. And the accusing eyes. 'Why?'

This was not the time for lengthy explanations. There was a commonplace expression, over-used to the point of being meaningless, but it was short so he gave it. 'It was him or me, missy.' Voiced, it sounded weak, like some whining pretext, but it was true. Red Toomey had been around some and knew the no-nonsense attitude of the bounty-hunter known as the Reaper. The chips down, the only choice was facing a rope or being gunned down by Grimm, unless he could somehow blast his way out of it. Which he had tried to do.

True or not, it didn't matter. She didn't hear. 'Why? Why?' In her eyes, for a moment, Grimm could see the sum of all the hate of all the kin and friends of every man he'd ever killed.

He looked around, tracking the environs with both gun barrels. There was nobody else. They'd have made their play by this time. He holstered his weapons.

Then, before he could stop her, she had two-handedly picked up one of her father's fallen guns and swung it in Grimm's direction. But the four and a half pounds of metal was too much for her and the barrel of the weapon wavered awkwardly as she sought to master its mechanism. He moved quickly forward and wrested it out of her delicate hands before she'd got the hang of using it. On her knees she pummelled at him with little fists. He didn't know what else he could say so he tried to cradle her head in his hand but she wrenched free. She pounded the sand until she found a stone and hurled it at him. It had no force and he let it hit him on the hip. Maybe the action would help take the top off her anger. She threw another ineffectively and then fell once more, sobbing on the dead man.

He shucked the cartridges from the chamber of the gun in his hand, then picked up the outlaw's second pistol. When it too was unloaded, he walked over to where his Andalusian was tethered and dropped the two weapons into a saddle-bag out of harm's way. He strolled back to the girl and rubbed the back of his skull as he watched her. He was prone to head pains when tension or bad emotion hit. And hell, it was hitting him now. Whatever Red Toomey deserved, the fact was Grimm had shot him dead in front of his daughter. Jeez, what a situation. Although a bounty-hunting killing machine when he had to be, Grimm still had some feelings.

He left her that way for several minutes, a pathetic sobbing bundle of homespun and calico. When the crying had become a snuffle, he helped her up. Arm around her narrow shoulders, he guided her into the shack. He sat her on the bed and hunkered down before her. 'What's your name, little girl?'

'Sarah.'

'That would be Sarah Toomey, wouldn't it?' he suggested. It figured. She'd got the same colour hair as the corpse outside. They hadn't called him Red for nothing.

She nodded.

'Well, Sarah,' he went on. 'What has happened here is terrible. I know that. I didn't want it to fall the way it did. But you gotta know the truth. Your pa was a wanted man. You know what that means, Sarah?'

She shook her head.

'Well, it means he'd done some real bad things and the law was after him. Sheriffs and stuff like that. It happens I was one of the men who was after him.'

'You a sheriff?' the girl asked, an iciness entering her voice.

'Kind of.' He rubbed his chin and his fingers rasped on stubble. 'Now, if your pa hadn't started shooting when I showed up ... maybe we could have worked something out. But he did start shooting. You heard it. That's a fact. If you was watching then you have see'd it all. And what happened, well it happened and can't be undone. So, we both gotta put that behind us and think about the future.' He looked around the shack. 'Ain't no rhyme in staying here for too long. You live with your ma?'

'Sometimes.'

'Well, we gotta get you back to her.'

She still didn't look at him. 'I don't want Ma. I want Pa.'

'That ain't possible now. Where's your ma live?'

'Abilene.'

'Abilene?' he queried, a groan evident in his voice. 'Abilene, Texas?'

She nodded.

Judas Priest, that was a few hundred miles away the last time he saw a map. 'That's a long ways away, Sarah. Don't you have any kin nearer?'

'No.' The voice was still icy.

He thought for a moment. 'Well, we can't stay here, that's for sure. We gotta head out.' He stood up while he thought some more. 'Don't worry, kid, we'll find someone to take care of you.' He glanced around to see if there were any more weapons. Even a small kid might be able to pull a trigger. But he couldn't see anything that could do any damage. 'OK. Now, you lie down a spell. I'll git the hosses ready.'

A half-hour had passed. He walked over to the table and picked up a warbag. Previously he'd asked her to gather together her possessions. 'Are all your things in here?'

'Yes.'

'Come on then, gal. Let's git going.' He walked outside and she followed.

'Is that ... Pa?' She pointed to the bundle lashed to the third horse. Grimm had wrapped the corpse in a tarp so there was no part of the body showing. 'Yes.'

'But he's got to be buried.'

He sighed and looked down the tree-covered hill. It was the timber country of the Ouachita Mountains. Hanging Judge Isaac Parker had initiated a new campaign to wipe out the legion of owlhoots who infested the Indian-held lands of Arkansas. Although the US Marshal's force had a complement of two hundred officers, so eager was the Judge to see the operation through quickly that he had made it known that he welcomed the help of bounty-hunters.* Presenting himself at Fort

* For Grimm's earlier work in Arkansas see 'Dollars for the Reaper' (Hale, 1990)

Smith, Grimm had been informed by the high sheriff that there was a pork barrel of six hundred dollars for anybody who fetched in Red Toomey or his partner Von Hoffman. Hoffman had disappeared somewhere along the line but Toomey was known to be holed up in the mountains. But, hell, nobody had said anything to him about the varmint toting his daughter.

'But Pa's got to be buried,' the girl repeated.

'He will be, gal. Later.'

'He's got to be buried now.' Her voice lowered as her mind went back. 'We found a dead sparrowhawk once, Ma and Pa, and we buried it right away. Put some flowers on the grave, said prayers. That's the proper way to do things. We gotta do that for Pa. Right away.'

'It don't work like that, Sarah.'

'It does so. I'm not leaving this place until Pa is buried properly.' She started to walk back to the shack. He shook his head in exasperation, then tied her pathetic little bundle of belongings to her horse and followed her inside.

She was sitting on the bed again. 'I'm not moving until we've done the proper thing with Pa.' There was a resolution in her voice that he was finding difficult to handle.

'Now listen, Sarah. We got a lot of riding to do. We're a long ways from anywheres. The sooner we start up the better. So act sensible.'

She didn't speak. It was plain that 'sensible' wasn't part of her vocabulary.

He looked at her. A pitiful little figure, bewildered, probably in shock. His plan of taking Toomey direct to Fort Smith was beginning to look unworkable. Maybe the plain fact was it wasn't even right to ask her to ride along with her father, dead and tarped up like that.

He put his hand on her shoulder. 'Wait here.' He moved away and rummaged through the detritus at the back of the shack. Sacking, broken tools, disintegrating wooden boxes. Eventually he came across a spade.

Outside, some distance from the building, he dug a grave. As a rule peace officers didn't like parting with money. They didn't see bounty payments as hard-earned and there was no way they would pay out without hard evidence, meaning the body. If the high sheriff at Fort Smith wanted to play the nit-picking bureaucrat, Grimm would have to return after he'd gotten shed of his little bundle of female trouble and come back to dig up the collateral. For this reason he made the grave a shallow one. Huh, what a way to earn a dollar. He laid the body, still tarped, in the hole.

When he had completed the operation out of the girl's view, he called her. She moved out into the sunlight and contemplated the mound, then said, 'There should be a cross.'

Jeez, a cross he had forgotten. 'Of course, miss.' Anything for a quiet life.

'Can you make one?' she asked, almost matter-of-factly.

'No problem, miss.'

'I shall collect some flowers while you make it.'

He found a piece of narrow planking in the shack and broke it in two. While he was lashing them crosswise with rawhide, he watched her. Moving between bushes and over the sward gathering flowers, she seemed, if not happy, at least unmindful of recent events. There were no longer any tears. The task of prettifying the grave had taken over.

Some time later they were standing before the bedecked grave. Grimm rubbed his throbbing head and suddenly realized how tired he was. He had been on Toomey's trail for over a week. The bastard had always been one jump ahead. Even now, it was the outlaw that was getting the rest while he stood exhausted, leaning on a shovel, sweat sticky under his armpits.

'We must say words,' she said. 'What do we say?'

Jonathan Grimm was momentarily nonplussed. He was more experienced in causing funerals than attending them. 'I only know the Lord's Prayer,' he said after he had racked his brain. She nodded sagely so he took off his hat and they recited together. On the 'Amen' she walked to the horse without another word and he helped her mount. They moved out, the three horses roped together. He glanced her way a few times when they had settled into their saddles and had moved some yards. There was no sadness in her face, she didn't even look back at the scene. It had become a game to her. She had been a child at play.

TWO

He reined in on a ridge and worked his shoulders. Long spells in the saddle made him stiff these days. Down below he could see a pool partially screened by brush and cottonwoods. He jerked on the tow rope and gigged his Andalusian, letting it find its own way down the grade. Near the trees he pulled in again and dismounted. 'Come on, gal. Time for a bath.'

Sarah didn't move as he stood, hands out-stretched to help her down. 'No,' was her only voicing.

'What do you mean – no? Everybody gotta wash regular. And especially young ladies.'

'Not here.'

'Ain't anywheres else, gal. When was the last time you bathed?'

'Dunno.'

'There you are then, little missy. All the more reason to have one now.' As he took her by the waist and yanked her to the ground, her proximity was overpowering to his nostrils. He'd already caught whiffs of her when the wind had been blowing his way during their journey. 'You be told: get stripped and into that water while I rustle up some chow. Don't worry. I ain't gonna look at yuh.'

Once freed from his grip she stomped across the sward and sat in the shade of a tree. He rummaged through a saddle-bag, took out a bar of soap and tossed it to her. Then from another he took out jerky, rye bread and the coffee makings. He laid them on the ground and set to gathering kindling for a fire. During these tasks, she remained immobile. 'Suit yourself,' he shouted, 'but I'm as sure as hell taking a bath when I've finished my chores here.' It had been a week since he had spent the night bedded down in a saloon. Huh, saloon had been too good a word for it: one-room shack with a liquor counter on one side and pallets on the other. And the bedsheets had been so thoroughly saturated with wood smoke from the goddamn fire permanently belching its fumes that he hadn't yet lost the odour. And he still itched from the bed-bugs.

She didn't move. He fingered the rye. It was as stale as hell and the jerky looked equally appetising. No sustenance for a growing child. Nor, come to that, for a bounty-hunter who should have been long pensioned off. 'Hell, I'm gonna see what fresh game I can pull,' he said looking towards the trees.

'You curse too much,' she said, school-ma'am disapprobation in her voice.

He harumphed in impatience, then had an idea. 'I'll strike a bargain with you, little lady. While I'm hunting you take a bath in yonder water and I'll stop using bad language.'

She remained unmoved.

'Listen,' he said in desperation. 'I'll admit I don't know too much about the feminine gender, but I do know one thing. They're supposed to smell purty. And smell purty, you don't.' With that he set off to the trees.

It was half an hour later. Whatever he had said, it had worked. She had bathed in the pool by the time he had returned with a brace of prairie-hens dangling from his fist. Then, while the critters had browned over the fire, he had taken to the water himself. Much to her amusement.

Later he was paring the delicate slivers of meat away from a leg bone with his teeth and watching the girl as he chewed. 'You don't get much substance from a bird,' he said, 'but it's better than stale bread and dry jerky, ain't it?'

He didn't get an answer; but he didn't need one. With her mouth and hands grease-shiny, she clearly relished the meal.

'You didn't tell me how long you'd been with your pa,' he prompted after another quiet spell.

'Since Sunday.'

'Since Sunday?' A calendar was not part of his kit so he wouldn't lay out a dollar on what day of the week it was, but her answer didn't sit right. 'You been with him longer than that,' he countered. 'That's only a few days and it's the best part of a month's ride to your ma's.' He hadn't told her that he had no intention of repeating that journey. He felt some responsibility for her, sure. But it ended at the point where he could off-load her some place appropriate. Other folk could get her back to her ma, if that was to be her course. 'How long you been with him?' he went on.

'Don't know. But it was Sunday when he came for me because the church bell was a-ringing.'

Grimm figured kids didn't have much sense of

time and left it at that. It wasn't important; he was
only making conversation over a meal. He threw the
last bone into the brush and wiped his lips before
looking back at her. 'Hey, you got a rent in your
dress,' he observed. 'I got a needle and thread
somewheres. I'll fix it.'

She twisted her dress and explored its folds until
she found the tear. 'I can do my own mending,
mister.'

'OK, gal. Sure is a good thing, looking after
yourself.'

Minutes later he was relaxing, puffing on his
corncob while she was fixing her dress. He observed
how the firelight caught her hair, endowing it with a
golden sheen. And how, with head bent forward
such that tresses spilled over her forehead, she
would now and again sweep them back so that she
could see to work.

'The son of a bitch!' she snapped suddenly and
rammed her finger in her mouth.

His eyes widened as the image of the little lady
dissipated. 'What's the matter, gal?'

'That's a dumb question! Stuck myself with the
goddamn needle is what.'

He was taken aback at the language. 'Hey, young
lady, what about our agreement about oathing?'

'That was for you not to curse,' she mumbled, her
mouth half full of blooded finger. 'Not me. Anyways, it was you said we got a bargain. Not me.'

He shook his head at his lack of understanding
the female psyche. This little missy was only about
ten years old, but already had more sides than a
conniving double-dealing possum. 'You sure I can't
finish off the job for you?' he offered.

'Hell, I ain't no helpless kid, you know,' she

replied, resuming her chore.

He exhaled smoke and watched it hang for a moment on the still air. 'Joshing apart, that language ain't becoming for a young lady. Especially one smelling as clean and fresh as you do.'

'You can't tell me nothing what to do. You ain't my pa.'

'You still gotta grow up proper. And that means listening to adults telling you what's what.'

She grunted before biting off the loose strand of twine.

He let her be, a spell. Then he said casually, 'You know you really should do as I bid you. I'm old enough to be your mother.'

She looked up and almost threw back one of her smart-ass comments when she realized what he had said. She returned to her sewing without a word; but Grimm could see a stifled smile.

They remained still, both in need of rest and the opportunity for their food to digest. 'How old are you really?' she asked after a spell.

'Little gals ain't supposed to ask questions like that.'

'Why not?'

'It ain't proper to ask after the age of growed-up folk.'

'You say that word a lot. Proper this and proper that. What do you mean 'proper'?'

'Hellfire, missy, you know what proper means.' But she kept her inquisitorial eye on him so he continued. 'There's things you should do and things you shouldn't do. Proper is the difference between them.'

She paused, then asked, 'Well, how old are you?'

ignoring the directly preceding conversation. 'You still ain't said.'

He breathed out loud in exasperation, flapping his grizzled jowls like a bull mastiff. Then, 'You got a grandpa?'

'Dunno. Reckon so.'

'Well, whether you got one or not, I'm as old as him. Now shut up.'

The silence following his last command was only brief. 'You sure look old.'

He nodded. That was true. He hadn't worn well, with the dried skin of his face manifesting a cobweb of fine criss-crossing lines. He was lean-framed and his cheeks were sunken giving him the gaunt aspect that accorded with the rubric of 'The Reaper' tagged on to him years ago by a fancifying smart-ass newspaper man.

'You as old as the ocean?' she went on.

He didn't cotton to this conversation. 'What in tarnation does that mean?'

'Had a teacher once, said the ocean was old.'

'Well, your teacher was right. But I ain't that old.'

'Have you ever see'd the ocean?'

'Sure.'

'Which one?'

'Pacific. Was in San Francisco once.'

'What was it like?'

He cut the air with a flattened palm. 'Flat like a desert. But blue. Richest blue I ever did clap eyes on.'

'I ain't never see'd the ocean.'

He snorted. 'You keep control of your trap, and stop exasperating folks, and you might grow up to see it one day.'

*   *   *

They'd been in the saddle all afternoon and the sun was now low. 'I gotta do things,' she suddenly said.

'What things?' he asked, still not tuned into the way children, especially female children, might speak.

'You know. Things.'

'Oh, yeah,' he said, the meaning dawning on his inflexible old brain. 'Things.' He took in the fading light. 'We gotta make camp anyhows. Look there's a place in the lee of those trees. A creek too.'

After he'd reined in, Sarah dismounted and scampered behind some bushes. He off-saddled and sat down to watch the horses cropping bunch grass in the half-light. Then he topped up the canteens from the creek and the two of them ate a little cornmeal with jerky washed down with water. He was too stiff and tired to rustle up a fire for coffee. He untied the bedrolls from the saddles and dropped one at her feet. 'Lay your bedroll flat and roll yourself up in it.'

'I know how to sleep, mister. Thank you very much.'

'Reckon you do at that,' he said.

They prepared their bedding placements in silence.

'Goodnight, Sarah,' he said, when they had finally bedded down.

He received no reply, grunted and immediately went to sleep himself.

THREE

Once out of timber country the sun-baked earth was as hard as iron and they had pounded it for two whole days when they hit a river. What track there was disappeared at the water's edge to reappear on the other side, indicating the river was fordable at some time. Grimm dismounted and went to the edge. He tried to estimate the depth but the water was muddy. 'Must have been rain upstream a piece,' he muttered. He studied the flow against the bank-side but couldn't detect any change in the level. If it was the result of distant rain, it could be rising or falling, so any advantage in waiting was unpredictable. 'Can you swim, Sarah?' he shouted back.

'No, sir,' came the reply.

He walked back to his horse. He knew there was enough rope in his saddle-bag to span the distance and there was a tree on the far side, but nothing on this to which to secure it.

'Stay here,' he said to the girl. He led his Andalusian to the edge and rubbed his hands before extracting the rope and uncoiling it. He anchored one end to the saddle-horn. 'Even more important, gal,' he said to his horse, patting its neck, 'you stay here too.' Then he tied the other end around his waist and waded in. He was lucky. Except for a few yards in the middle his feet kept contact with the river-bed. Knowing he was anchored and couldn't be swept too far down stream he threw himself into swimming the short distance, making it on the second attempt. On the far side he tied the rope to the tree and worked his way back.

Sarah was watching apprehensively, having moved some distance back. 'I'm not going across there,' she said as he approached.

'You have to, miss. You can't stay here and, one way or another, you're gonna have to cross this river. Now, don't be scared. All you have to do is hang on to me.'

He led her slowly by the hand into the water and she faltered when the water deepened and her dress ballooned with the uprush of water.

'You're doing fine, miss,' he said. 'Now hold tight on to me. We won't get swept away 'cos I'm holding the rope, see?'

She screamed when they reached the deep section and she felt his body drop then float away from the river-bed. 'Only a short spell,' he managed to shout back. They swung a few yards off centre but soon hit the bed. Another five minutes and they were across.

'Wasn't so bad, was it?' he asked when they were safely on solid ground, water dripping from their clothes. She didn't speak but dropped to the ground and gripped the grass as though for security. She stayed that way, unmoving, watching him return for the horses.

He rode the second horse first. The deep middle

section was less daunting for the animal being taller and it didn't need telling which direction to go in as its hooves temporarily left the river-bed. On the final crossing an insecure saddle-bag drifted off the back of the Andalusian part way across. He made a grab for it but without success. The task complete and the horses tethered he stood at the river-bank looking in vain downriver for the bag, trying to remember what was in it. It was only a small thin one, so its contents couldn't have been too important.

'This is like an adventure, ain't it, Mr Grimm?' Sarah said as he returned. He took off his boots, upending them to tip out their unwelcome contents.

'It sure is,' he grunted. 'Now let's make a fire. We've got some clothes to dry.'

It was late afternoon when they hit a town. Sarah hadn't spoken for a long time. She was slumped in the saddle, a kid on a man's horse. God knows how she'd made the journey out this way with her old man. Couldn't have been leisurely, him being wanted and all. Likely, she'd been dragged, just like Grimm was doing with her.

So the scatteration of clapboard buildings that called itself a town was welcome. Small, but maybe big enough to hold a solution to his problem. When he left this burg he intended that he would leave his responsibilities behind also. He squinted to read the signs down both sides of the street, noting the one proclaiming the marshal's office. There was a guy with a badge seated on the verandah of the building. Grimm nodded to the lawman as they passed.

He pondered on his next move. He decided against approaching the marshal. Chances were he could stir up some kind of hornets' nest if he brought the law into this business with the kid and the killing of her father. They passed a saloon. A drinking-parlour was usually a good place for information but bar-room drunks would not be the best folk for advising him on any local amenities for looking after a young girl. Then he saw a draper's store. There was likely to be women in there. They'd be the most sympathetic. But what to do with Sarah while he made enquiries? He knew he would stir up a hornets' nest for sure if she heard the conversation he planned to have so he reined in outside a grocery store.

He dropped down and secured the horses, then helped his self-appointed responsibility to dismount. He took a dollar from his pocket and pushed it into her hand. 'Get yourself some of that candy,' he said, pointing to a jar of brightly coloured confectionery in the window. 'Then stay here like a good gal till I come back. Won't be long.'

He watched her enter the store then he moved across the street to the draper's. Inside there were bolts of variously-coloured material stacked on shelves and the whole place smelled of new cloth. Sure enough, there was a woman behind the counter and a female customer.

The one behind the counter, a young lady of rotund build, was holding up some lace for inspection. She had slender fingers that didn't match her dumpy body and, at the moment, the fingers of one hand were tracing out the finery of the material's patterning. The customer was an older woman, rather tall, with questioning eyes and black hair like a skull-cap.

'Excuse me, ladies,' he said, taking off his hat. 'I was wondering if either of you two good womenfolk could help me.'

'What can we do for you?' the proprietress responded, lowering the lace. The customer stepped back, eyes piercing him and mouth firmly down-turned indicating her displeasure at the interruption.

'I've just rode into town. Along the trail I came across a young girl who seems to have lost her folk. Some accident out in the wild country. Anyways, she was all alone, so I brung her in. I'm a stranger in these parts and I ain't familiar with the set-up around here. And I can't just dump her anywheres. Do you know of someone who would take the stray in? A charity place or something like that?'

The older woman sniffed as an expression of not wanting anything to do with the trail-grimed stranger and his problem; but the plump one showed more understanding. 'Where is the little mite now?' she asked, pushing the lace to one side and moving round the counter.

'Outside. I've sent her for some candy while I came in here.'

'Well, let's begin by having a look at the little darling,' the proprietress said walking towards the door. 'I'm Mrs Ryan. My husband and I run the store here.'

'Pleased to meet you, ma'am,' the bounty-hunter said, following her. 'Grimm's my name.'

'What about my order?' the older woman asked stiffly, remaining by the counter.

'See if there's anything else you want while I'm

gone, Mrs Miller,' Mrs Ryan shouted back. 'I shouldn't be too long.'

'Name's Sarah,' Grimm said as they approached the horses and he could see Sarah had returned, her mouth sticky with candy.

'Hello, Sarah,' the lady said. 'My name's Mrs Ryan and your friend, Mr Grimm, has been telling me about you.'

The girl sucked on her candy without speaking.

'What do you think?' Grimm said. 'Think you could accommodate her until some arrangements can be made?'

'Of course. We have room. I'm sure something can be worked out. There are many families in and around the town. What belongings does she have?'

'Just what she stands in.'

'That's not a problem. Running a drapery, I can soon fix her up with new clothes.' She looked her charge up and down. 'But first, the tub, young lady.'

'Bye, Sarah,' Grimm said, touching the girl's shoulder. She maintained her silence as he watched her walk away, hand in hand, with the woman.

Talk of the tub reminded Grimm he could benefit from a freshening-up, but first a drink. He walked along the street to the saloon. It was a dingy place with a rough-hewn bar. He bought a beer and took it to a chair across the room. The hard wooden chair was luxury compared with the saddle. He quaffed most of the beer in one go, then lit his pipe.

By habit he had sat facing the entrance which is why he saw the skull-cap lady's head appear briefly over the batwings; but he gave it no mind. He finished his drink and returned to the bar. After his mug had been replenished he strode back to his chair, passing a man who had just entered. He didn't pay the newcomer much attention either, merely noting he wore a star. The lawman lingered at the bar, then disappeared to Grimm's right. But what he was aware of a short spell later was the voice that said, 'Don't move, mister' and the heavy click of a pistol being cocked as its muzzle poked into his back. A hand took his guns.

'What's this?' he asked through his clenched pipe stem.

'I'm the marshal and I've got some questions need answering. Now move your keester over to the law office nice and quiet.'

'Some welcome,' Grimm said, downing the remains of his drink and rising. His questions were ignored as he crossed the street under the inquisitive gaze of passers-by.

'It's come to my attention,' the marshal said when they were seated in the law office, 'that there's a young girl over at Mrs Ryan's.'

'Who told you that?'

'Never mind.' Grimm figured it would be the skull-cap female with the permanent on-the-prod look. Not that it mattered now. 'What's more,' the lawman continued, 'the little girl says you killed her pa. That true?'

'Sure. I got nothing to hide. He was Red Toomey and he was a wanted man. You must have his likeness amongst your dodgers.'

The marshal glanced at the array of wanted posters pinned on the wall. 'Never heard of him.'

'Well, the son-of-a-bitch was wanted for a whole string of jobs, banks, murder. I'm a bounty-man and I'd been trailing him for weeks. Finally tracked him down to a cabin in the Ouachita Mountains. Anyways, he didn't take kindly to being taken into custody. I had to shoot him when he resisted arrest and started blasting. My slug caught him bad and he died; regrettable but it happens sometimes.'

'You got any documents proving some of these things?'

'Sure. I got papers with my name on. And his dodger amongst others.'

'Where?'

'In my saddle-bag.'

'We been through your things. Nothing.'

They sure work fast here, he thought. Then he remembered the bag disappearing down the river. At the time he'd tried to recall its contents but dismissed it as being unimportant. Huh, now it came to him. It contained his papers. His face took on the aspect of a school kid confronted with some misdemeanour. 'Jehosophat, I lost them crossing the river on the way to town.'

'Yeah,' the marshal said cynically. 'Convenient.'

The Reaper's wrinkled face became serious. He didn't like whining to some penny-ante badge carrier. 'I am what I say. Jonathan Grimm. Bounty collecting is my trade. You can check with the authorities in Fort Smith. That's probably the nearest place from here where I've had dealings. They'll remember doing business with me. They'll have my signature on receipts in their files.'

'Sure, I can check, but by itself that won't mean nothing. Them's just words. Any no-good would know the name of a bounty-hunter and where he operates. You could be anybody.'

'OK, ask 'em for a physical description of me. They'll oblige you with that. And there ain't many riding an Andalusian, like I got out there. That should clinch it.'

The marshal paused. 'If you're a bounty-hunter like you say, where did you check Toomey's body in?'

'I didn't. I buried it. Out there, by the cabin in the Ouachitas.'

The lawman sniggered. 'I ain't never heard of a bounty burying the body. Either you don't know the rules of your own game, or you're lying in your teeth.'

'I was thinking of the girl's feelings. The man I'd killed was her pa.'

'Sure,' the marshal said, 'a dollar-grabbing bounty-hunter with a heart!' He rose and, still keeping his gun on Grimm, collected keys from a hook. 'Well, while I check what I can, you're staying in the slammer.'

Grimm shrugged and stood up. He realized how the mess of circumstances could look suspicious. He could be up a tree. In fact, the more he thought about it, the more he realized that in a small town and the only thing known about him was the killing of a little gal's pa, he could soon be up a tree in a more literal sense.

FOUR

Sarah refused to get in the tub. Mrs Ryan was a mother-hen of a woman and was prepared to show forebearance to the child given what she had gone through. As much as for the child she had indulged herself in taking her in. But she was becoming worried about how her husband would react. They hadn't had children because he couldn't stand them. She hadn't found that out until they were married and now it was too late. Despite her time being taken up during the day with running the drapery store, the house was clean and well kept because that's the way he insisted it should be. Children would not fit into that way of living. He had a poison temper and would rant should he find anything out of its allotted place, as it was. Thus, she wanted the little girl to be quiet and presentable when he came home from the land office where he worked as a clerk.

Meg Miller, the customer in the shop when Grimm had entered, had accompanied Mrs Ryan to the apartment when she had taken the child. So she had been there when Mrs Ryan had questioned the girl and had tutted noisily at the answers about

guns and killing. Mrs Ryan knew her as a busybody
and that she was suspicious about the circumstances but hadn't expected her to go straight to
the marshal on leaving.

The lawman had called when she was filling the
tub and asked Sarah the same questions. All they
could get from her was that the stranger who had
brought her in had shot her father and they had
buried him up in the hills. The lawman had quickly
left without stating his intentions.

She looked at the clock on the wall. 'Come on,
Sarah,' she said and lapped the water with her
fingers. 'We want to be nice and clean like a pretty
girl should be, don't we? Then we can put these
new clothes on.' But the youngster was adamant,
sitting stiff-lipped on a chair by the fire, paying no
attention to the tub or the flowered dress laid out
on the table.

Mrs Ryan stiffened when she heard a noise at the
door. It was her husband and his entry was without
greeting for his wife. All he said was 'What's this?'
when he saw the child. His wife explained.

'How many times have I told you, woman, that
we do not run a home for waifs and strays? Any
dog or cat that comes whining at the door you take
in.' The ends of his mouth were turned down as he
appraised the child. 'Dirty, too.'

'I'm trying to get her to bathe,' Mrs Ryan said.
'But she's in strange surroundings. You must
expect her to be uncertain of things and reluctant
to do what is requested of her.'

'Woman, it is not required of me to expect
anything.'

'Anyway, she'll only be here for a little while, till
things get sorted out.'

'Won't even be for a little while. I'm not having a child in my house. A dirty one too. Look, the grime will get everywhere. You can't put something like that between clean sheets.'

'Have a little Christian charity, Jim.'

Ignoring her, he moved forward and took Sarah's arm. 'Come on, child. The marshal can handle this. It's his job not ours.'

Through the jail window, the buildings at the end of town were silhouetted against the darkening sky and the street was devoid of folk save for the occasional night-owl making his way to a drinking-parlour. Grimm got back on his bunk and tried to sleep but the crickets were just starting up their goddamned chirping.

There was a commotion at the door. He moved so he could observe. He recognized Sarah and the woman he knew as Mrs Ryan. The unfamiliar man accompanying them did all the talking and it soon transpired he was Mr Ryan.

'So you see, Marshal,' Ryan went on like a cold, glassy-eyed fish, 'the child cannot stay with us. A matter such as this is your responsibility. That's why we pay taxes.'

'Where can I put the kid at this time of night?' the lawman pressed.

'That is your concern, not mine.' Ryan looked beyond the man's shoulder. 'You got a spare cell back there, ain't yuh?'

'A prison isn't the place for the poor mite,' Mrs Ryan said.

'Shut up, woman,' her husband snapped. 'Time for us to go.'

'Hold on there,' the marshal said. 'Ain't she got

any folks at all?'

'It appears her mother lives in Abilene,' Mrs Ryan said.

The marshal looked at Sarah as he pondered on the tale. She was kicking the wall, slowly but powerful hard. Then he said, 'Seems to me the kid should go to her ma.'

'That's for you to figure, Marshal,' Ryan said, his hand going to the door knob. 'Be my guest.'

'Jeez,' the lawman pondered, 'that's a helluva long ways off.'

'The Lord be thanked for small mercies,' Ryan said smugly. 'We have a marshal with some knowledge of geography.'

'The way the kid talks about her ma,' Grimm said from the rear, 'she'd have to be dragged there in chains. She don't wanna go. And believe me she can be an ornery cuss. Got a mind of her own. I've learned that much.'

'Stow it,' the marshal shouted back. 'Who's asking your opinion?'

The marshal looked at the girl again. There was powdered adobe on the floor where she was still toeing the wall. Every now and again she would look their way. The lawman had faced up to a mess of hardcases in his time but he didn't cotton one bit to the mean look she was throwing his way.

'Looks a handful all right,' he observed. His mind was countenancing the prospect of being saddled with the young female maverick.

Grimm was enjoying this. From the cell he said loudly, 'I know the gal, Marshal. I don't think I'd have to swear an affidavit for you to believe that she can be hell on wheels for a little 'un.'

The marshal ignored the comment. 'Ain't no

place local that I could take her. Town's made mainly of men folk.' An extra seriousness came to his face as he thought on it. He would have to come up with something to get the pair of them off his hands. 'And ain't right to put a kid in a cell.'

'Seems to me,' the clerk said with a sneer, 'given her parentage, it's quite appropriate.' With that he took his wife's arm and firmly escorted her out of the building.

The marshal turned from the closed door. He looked perplexed, then he spoke. 'No, missy, don't seem fitting for you to bed down in there.'

He raised a fist to the side of his face with all the appearance of going to punch it in exasperation but then the little finger stuck out from his balled hand and he chewed its nail. 'But in the circumstances,' he went on, 'ain't nothing for it. Still there's a pallet and I can get some extra blankets to make it softer for you. We'll have to arrange better accommodation for you some-wheres else in the morning. Lord knows, where.' She had become inactive and was leaning against the wall, sucking her thumb as he walked towards the cell. 'Come on, missy.'

She hesitated but sleep was grabbing at her eyelids and she complied.

'Hi there, Sarah,' Grimm said as she passed his cell.

'Now shut up, you,' the marshal snapped, turning on the prisoner. 'You've said enough already. And don't talk to the gal neither while she's in here. Or you'll spend the night chained up outside like the dog you probably are.'

Sarah entered the compartment apprehensively, her heavy-lidded eyes taking in the accoutrements:

the pallet, the barred window, the bucket in the
corner.

'Don't worry, kid,' the man said as he lifted her up
to sit on the pallet, 'I'll leave the door open.' Then he
went to fetch blankets.

It was pushing midnight when roustabouts on their
way home from the saloon passed the jail singing
and joshing each other. Grimm hadn't gone to sleep
but he looked through the bars and noted the noise
had awakened Sarah. 'It's OK, kid,' he said. 'Only
young men funning. You can go back to sleep.' But
she sat up. The marshal had left the kerosene
burning and she looked blankly around the interior
of the small building. The puzzlement left her eyes
when she realized where she was. 'Nothing to worry
about,' Grimm went on. 'Just lie down and snuggle
back under the blanket.'

'I've told you not to talk,' came the reminder from
the marshal. 'There's still time to chain you up
outside.'

'Kid needs pacifying and you weren't doing it.'
Grimm stood up and held the bars of his door.
'Anyways, I need to relieve myself. How about
letting me out a spell?'

'What you think the bucket's for? You've used it
before.'

'Yeah, that was before occupancy was taken up in
the next cell.'

'What the hell you on about?'

Grimm looked at Sarah. She had lain down but
her eyes were still open. 'Ain't right to undertake
such things in front of the girl.'

'Do it, or hold it,' the marshal grunted.

'Judas Priest, what else should I expect from

small-town hicks?'

'Who you calling a small-town hick?'

'Then do the decent thing and open the door. You got that big iron, ain't yuh? I ain't gonna do anything stupid with that trained on me.'

'Yeah,' the marshal conceded, standing up and reaching for his keys. 'And I'll blow your pecker off if you give me any trouble.' At the door he put the key in the lock. 'Stand back and bring your bucket with yuh. It stinks to high heaven as it is.'

The lawman stepped back, his pistol levelled, its muzzle indicating for Grimm to come out. Grimm stepped round the bars and moved past a corner in the brickwork. Out of sight of the girl, he made to place the bucket on the ground but, before he had completed the expected action, his second hand gripped the rim and he jerked it upwards. The metal edge whacked the gun muzzle upwards while the contents, already a quarter of the pail's capacity, hit the lawman in the face, the rim continuing in its upwards motion to catch him under the chin.

The unfortunate law officer stumbled off balance and before he could take any retaliatory action the Reaper had smashed the pail down on his skull. The erstwhile prisoner grabbed the fallen gun and held it in readiness but there was no immediate need. The man was out cold, his face and clothes drenched in rancid urine.

Grimm went to the office section of the building passing Sarah who had come from her cell at the sound of the commotion. 'What you doing?' she asked as he slung the bolt across the door.

'Don't worry. I ain't hurt him. It was necessary to put him out, is all.'

'What you doing?' she repeated.

'Lighting out,' he said as he took a coil of rope from a hook. 'You get yourself back to bed. Somebody is bound to pass by in the morning and see to your looking after. You can unlock the door at sun-up.'

'I don't want to stay here. I don't like anybody in this town.'

'Ain't nothing for it but for you to stay here, missy.' He ignored the girl and set about binding the unconscious man. Tying critters up was part-and-parcel of his trade so it was a thorough job, the lawman's hands and legs transfixed, the ankles brought backwards with the final length.

'Take me with you,' she said, watching him ransack cupboards. Finally he found a cloth which he rammed in the man's mouth. The man grunted but didn't awaken.

'You're only a kid.' He collected his guns and other belongings. 'You don't understand.'

'All right, I'll scream. Somebody will come and you won't get away.'

He stopped in his tracks and looked at her, his grey eyes serious. The first thing that crossed his mind was to gag and bind her like the lawman. No problem, missy, he thought. Then he realized he really couldn't do that.

His silence prompted her to walk towards the door. Jumping Jehosophat, the little tyke meant it. He stayed her arm. 'OK, what you want me to do?'

'Take me with you.'

He was nonplussed. Then he conceded, 'Very well, but be quiet, will yuh?' He breathed heavy in frustration. He'd never been railroaded by anyone so small in his life.

FIVE

Despite the fact Grimm could now have the charge of kidnapping added to that of murder they travelled slow. They only had the horses they rode and he didn't want to ride them into the ground or have one break a leg wrong-footing in the dark. They made the same ambling pace throughout the night with Sarah's horse in tow and him glancing back in the moonlight to make sure she hadn't fallen asleep and out of the saddle. Come dawn he found a cave and they slept the morning away hidden from view.

For two days they journeyed in such a fashion. For the next two he chanced more daylight riding, staying clear of settlements, eating what he brought down with his rifle and sleeping under the stars. On the fifth day he spotted a wagon train nooning beside a gravelly creek. He pulled rein before a knoll and took out his field-glasses. A dozen ox-led prairie schooners and a handful of four-horse freight wagons.

As he lowered the glasses against his chest and considered his next course of action he noticed his companion eyeing the glasses with open curiosity.

'Ever looked through a pair of these things?' he said.

She shook her head. He took the loop from around his neck and handed them to her. 'Lie down on the grade here to steady yourself and have a look-see.'

'Looks like they're headed west,' he said when she had settled herself with the instrument. 'They could be a help. That's the direction you want to go in.'

She said nothing as they mounted up and rode at an angle towards the halted caravan. Confident that the folk would not have had access to any news and therefore would not know of his circumstances, he reined in near a camp-fire. After exchanging greetings with the travellers, he asked for the wagonmaster. While a teamster went to locate him, Grimm noticed a bunch of children at play. He pointed out some girls with dolls and nudged Sarah in their direction.

He took some coffee and entered into conversation with those around the fire. As he learned they were out of Independence, Missouri, making for California, he saw the teamster returning. Alongside him was a tall fellow with a bearing that suggested time spent in the military, probably a cavalry regiment. His army experience was endorsed by the way he was introduced by the teamster. 'This is the Captain, head of the train.'

'You looking for me, stranger?' The wagon-master's face was haggard and he revealed receding hair as he took off his wide-brimmed hat to wipe a bony brow.

'Howdy,' Grimm said. 'From what these good folks tell me you'll be heading through Texas?'

'If the good Lord is willing.'

Grimm pointed to Sarah who was investigating one of the children's dolls. 'The young girl over there. I found her wandering alone on the trail. Nothing for it but to pick her up. I've got it out of her that she has relatives in Texas.' Once more he had decided against giving the actual circumstances of his involvement lest it unnecessarily complicated the situation. 'But Texas ain't on my route and I ain't the best bozo in the world for looking after a kid. It would be doing her a service if you found her a space on your train and dropped her off that way.'

The wagonmaster shook his head. 'I'm afraid we couldn't oblige, mister.'

'She ain't any kin of mine but I could pay something for the inconvenience.'

'Money's no good out here.'

'Then what else can I offer?'

'It's not a matter of what you can give us. It's just plumb out of the question.' He waved a hand at the wagons. 'Times have been bad the last hundred miles,' he continued wearily. 'We have sickness amongst our number and are down on food supplies.'

'Sorry to hear that,' Grimm said. The burden of such problems helped explain the haggard look to the wagonmaster's face.

'In these conditions,' the man went on, 'we could not take on an extra responsibility. The fact that you have taken her on board shows that you have the necessary compassion. And, by her look, you have clearly tended well to the child and are far more capable than we to see to her immediate needs. But you are welcome to share coffee before continuing your journey.'

Grimm could see there was little point in pushing his request any further. 'Thanks, mister.'

'Now, if you'll excuse me, I have things to attend to. I wish you a safe passage wherever you are going.' With that the leader returned the hat to his head and walked down the train.

Grimm settled down to another mug of coffee and passing-the-day conversation with those around the fire. In their faces and demeanour he could now see the effects of poor diet.

'Sure was good of you to take her under your wing, pardner,' one of their number said. 'Some guys wouldn't have taken on the burden. Pity we can't be of help.'

'Like your boss said, she's probably best with me as it stands,' Grimm concluded. He finished off his pipe and was just about to call Sarah so that they could leave when excited words were exchanged between a young man and woman close by.

'It just occurred to me,' the young man said to Grimm, 'we passed a place some time ago that might be of help to you in your predicament.'

'Yeah, what's that?'

'It was a sign on the trail, a short ways from a settlement.' The man's features had brightened. 'I'd paid it no mind but my missus just remembered it. Pointed to an orphanage as we recall.'

Grimm was interested. 'What was the location?'

He thought a spell. 'Dunno, but was about a day back down the trail.'

Another was screwing up his features while he still cast his mind around for the name. Then he came up with, 'Tucker's Gap. That was it, pardner.'

'I'm much obliged folks,' Grimm said, rising and

knocking out his smouldering dottle. 'Seems like I might have a solution to my problem after all.'

A quarter of an hour later, he and Sarah were back in the saddle, the wagon train and its unfortunate folk well to their rear. 'I know of some people – good people – who are used to looking after kids,' he said to the girl. 'They'll be happy to give you a home.'

'Where?' she asked, her mouth full of the remains of a candy stick she had found.

'Place called Tucker's Gap.'

'Don't wanna go.'

He looked back. Jesus, he thought. This kid! Her face was moulded by determination and an expression deriving from the confidence that she held some kind of power over him and the situation. The hell she did. Why, he could just ride the hell out and leave her. Yeah. But he thought on it some more. No, who was he kidding? He couldn't do that. The little maverick did have some kind of hold on him in a strange way; and she knew it. Jeez. He felt that twinge of tension in his head again.

'There's some nice folks there,' he said, embarrassed and irritated to note an unnatural pleading tone had entered his voice.

'Who?'

'Don't know their names, but they run an orphanage.'

'I ain't no orphan!'

'Talk sense, kid!' Grimm snapped, his contrived patience evaporating. Then he pulled himself in check. 'Look, it's real sad you ain't got no pa. That's a fact, whatever the cause. But we gotta look at reality. I know you don't wanna stay with me and, anyways, you can't. You keep telling me you don't wanna go back to the ma that you've got left, Lord know why. It's best for a growing kid to be with kin. But you got your reasons and I respect that. So, it's gotta be folk like I told you about. They come well recommended so it'll a proper place. There'll be decent meals, a bath, a soft comfortable bed, stuff like that.'

She remained sullen as he turned to look ahead. 'Now, finish your candy,' he went on, 'while I look for a place for the night. Then we head out at sun-up.'

SIX

Grimm was cursing under his breath. Tucker's Gap was further along the back-trail than the youthful pioneer had estimated. It had taken them over three days ride to reach it. Three days in which to get more saddle sore, further torture ancient joints, rattle each other's nerves and fill lungs with trail dust.

He had spied the settlement first. It was small and without telegraph wires. Just what he wanted. Meant no news about his escapades and jailbreak would have come ahead of him. Enquiries had led him to the large clapboard house bearing the sign ORPHANAGE FOR YOUNG GENTLELADIES. PROPRIE-TORS: MR AND MRS MCCAREY.

He looked at the young 'gentlelady' sitting beside him. Couldn't really tell whether it was a girl or a boy. 'Tidy your hair, kid,' he said. 'Make yourself look presentable.'

Sarah remained impassive. He leant across and tried to smooth her hair with his gnarled hand but she pulled away. He dropped down, tethered the horses, then helped her to the ground. Her face, like his, was grimy with trail mess. He took out a handkerchief, spat on it and, with some difficulty

47

due to her resistance, rubbed her face. But he only succeeded in turning the uniform dirt into a series of unsightly smears which, decorating a face now screwed up with the repugnance of his action and eyes piercing malevolently through a drapery of tangled hair, had about as much appeal to a prospective custodian as dog droppings.

He shook his head and advanced to the door, realizing the pair now had an audience as he caught sight of young inquisitive noses pressed against the windows. Other young gentleladies. He glanced back to see Sarah sticking out her tongue at the onlookers. He shook his head again and hoped the proprietors weren't watching her. Judas Priest, he would have to play this thing coolly if he was to get the little varmint off his hands once and for all.

He knocked at the door which eventually opened. Cheerfully he made himself known to the couple, both of whom came to the door, visitors to their establishment being a rarity. Mr McCarey had much the air and attire of a preacher while his wife was a comely matron of superior stature to her spouse. Grimm remained in the doorway as he gave them a brief version of the girl's story, omitting any reference to Sarah's father being a criminal lest it act against the chances of her acceptance.

'The poor girl's father quietly expired after a short illness,' he whispered in conclusion, giving no indication that the shortness of the illness had been a mere fifteen seconds and could be diagnosed as lead poisoning.

'You would like to see something of our facilities, of course,' Mrs McCarey prompted, 'before you make a decision.'

'Of course,' Grimm said, taking off his hat when

the couple stepped back as an invitation to enter. He beckoned to Sarah to accompany him. He forcibly gripped her hand so that she couldn't get into mischief as they were shown the kitchen and cramped bunkrooms. Here and there, as the party made its way around the building, girls dressed in the long calico dresses deferentially and silently stepped out of their way. Out back, young girls of a variety of ages up to around fourteen years were involved in washing clothing.

'We make sure all our children do their turns with the chores,' Mrs McCarey explained. 'Makes sure they are capable of looking after themselves when the time comes.' She turned to Sarah and put her hand on the girl's head. 'Stay here, child, and watch the other girls while we talk with your guardian.'

Grimm winked at Sarah as he was shown back inside but her look had 'traitor' across it. The three adults stepped into the dining-room. It was a large room with whitewashed walls and ceiling. There was a long deal table with two rough-hewn benches on either side. A rude chandelier made of two laths fixed crosswise with candles held in by nails was suspended from the ceiling.

'The food is plain fare but nutritious,' Mrs McCarey said. 'The children take baths twice a week and attend church on Sundays. Mr McCarey and I are very keen church-folk.'

'What about schooling?' Grimm asked, finding he was unexpectedly developing the role of surrogate parent.

'We teach them their letters and numbers here. We have a schoolroom on the premises. I know something of literature and Mr McCarey's specialty is history.'

Grimm felt like he should ask some more questions but he didn't know what. He shuffled his boots, then asked, 'How long you been established here, ma'am?'

'Three years next fall. Not long you may think, but if you have concern for our standing in the community, ask anyone hereabouts. In our relatively short time we have developed a reputation, a reputation for giving the children in our charge, love and care.'

He nodded.

'I know conditions are sparse,' she added, 'Even Spartan one might say. But I can assure you we mean nothing but good, Mr Grimm.'

'I'm sure you do, ma'am. In the circumstances I don't think the kids could ask for more.' In awkwardness he ran the rim of his hat through his fingers for its whole circumference, coughed, then said, 'Well, I reckon I'll be moving on then, ma'am.'

'Do you wish to say goodbye to Sarah?'

In his mind's eye he had the image of her accusing face as he had winked to her out back. 'Naw. We already made our parting, in a manner of speaking. She wouldn't thank me for it. Anyways, she and me didn't hit it off.' As he got to the door he pulled a fold of bills from his pocket. A hundred dollars. He figured that was how much he'd get for Red Toomey's horse and rig. 'You'll take that, ma'am, towards her keep?'

The lady looked at the bills and shook her head. 'Oh no, we don't take money with the children. That would be mercenary. What we do here is our vocation in life, Mr Grimm.'

He was nonplussed. The folks he ordinarily met up with wouldn't give the big no to cash, especially not a C's worth of the folding green. But he couldn't keep it. He would feel guilt. It rightly belonged to Sarah. 'Is there anything against you taking the cash as a general donation?'

Mrs McCarey smiled and finally accepted the money. 'You're very kind, Mr Grimm. Yes, we are a charity.'

And with that, he took his leave.

SEVEN

He felt like some goddamn stone had been lifted from his shoulders. The last week had been a strain. He had lived so long by himself he didn't take too kind to having to think about the needs of another – feeding, resting, bathing, washing clothes. Especially a back-answering kid. He'd got ninety dollars for Toomey's horse and rig. He was ten dollars down. What the hell? It was only money and the whole business was behind him now. All he had to do was pick up the pieces. To be precise, dig up old Red, get the bounty on the critter, then get the hell out.

When he finally got back to the cabin up in the Ouachitas he didn't have to dismount to learn the situation, but he did. He'd already taken in the scene, namely the gaping hole, on his approach. He hitched his horse and walked over to the empty cavity. Some bastard had already been busy with the spade, the instrument now carelessly thrown to one side – and Red Toomey's corpse was gone.
    Who'd done that? Another bounty-hunter? Toomey sure-as-hell hadn't dug himself up. From what he knew of the renegade, he'd had resilience,

an ability to bounce back, a quality he had passed on to his daughter. But even Toomey couldn't bounce back from the Big One. No, it had to be a dodger-hunter. There was enough of them about, attracted by the green stuff Judge Parker was promising. Or maybe just a plain opportunist. There was plenty of them about too. Either way, Grimm was coming up with an empty bag.

He looked for sign. Couldn't read any apart from a few scuffed stones. The ground was too rocky. But he didn't need printed directions nor a college diploma to work it out. If the bozo who had done the disinterring was in the business he would have hauled the body to Fort Smith to claim payment. And that was the way Grimm would head.

But what was the rush? He looked at the cabin. It held the promise of coffee and a few provisions. If not, he could use the facilities to prepare fare from his saddlebag and rest up. As he stepped onto the verandah, he remembered Sarah standing in the doorway and how he had nearly shot her. Bad memories.

He stepped out of the office labelled High Constable. That was what they called the chief law officer in Fort Smith. Grimm rubbed his temple and grunted to himself in an exasperated resignation. He stood on the boardwalk unseeingly watching the folks going about their business up and down the street. Knowing Grimm, the constable had been obliging when he had enquired about Toomey being brought in. The varmint had been brung in all right. By Lee Hammersley. That was another bone he had to pick with that scavenger when he met up with him.

But there would be no point in looking for the critter. It was more than an even chance Hammersley knew that it had been Grimm who had shown the outlaw the big exit sign, and he would have lit out from Fort Smith with the cash – and a big smile on that ugly face of his.

Then Grimm's features relaxed and he smiled philosophically. There was plenty of time to settle the score with Hammersley. Sharing the same line of business their trails had crossed many times; and there was more than an even chance they would do so again.

He'd told the constable of his contretemps with the marshal over Toomey's shooting way back and the officer had promised to wire the law office there and square Grimm with them in case he ever returned.

He tapped his open palm with the rolled-up papers he held in his hand, half-a-dozen dodgers the constable had given him. There was a few months' work there, OK. The one who interested him was a bank-robber and all-round no-good who went by the name of Von Hoffman. From what the constable had told him he could be the nearest, as the buzzard flies, some hundred miles west. The scuttle-butt was he was thought to be heading for Yellowrock, a makeshift town at the foot of the Wiseman Hills. Seems the place had sprung up following the unearthing of a gold vein by some poke the previous season. A new sprawling mining camp would have no law-and-order, a perfect place for a wanted man to hole up in a spell. Feeling secure, he probably wouldn't be expecting a bounty hunter.

But Grimm was stove up. He stuffed the reward

posters into his inside pocket and headed in the
direction of a cheap boarding-house he knew of.

He headed out at daybreak the next morning.
He was off regular trails so it was nightfall when he
at last hit a town. Dismounting he led his tired
Andalusian up the main street. He could hear
voices and a tinkling piano. Judas Priest, could he
do with a drink. He watered his horse, tethered it
then stepped in the direction of the beckoning
sounds.

Eventually an imposing false front loomed
bearing the legend:

SUEZ SALOON
PROPRIETRESS: SUZANNE FELICITY RANDALL

He pushed through the batwings under the sign
to be greeted by the tinkle of glassware, music, the
smell of booze and the flat rumble of talk. After a
couple of months on the trail, this was civilization.
The air was thick with smoke. Just the way he liked
it. There was only so much fresh, clean air a man
could take. Through the haze he could make out
the walls decorated with Egyptian motifs: fox-
headed gods, pharoahs on thrones. He remembered the Suez bit on the sign outside.

He got himself a jug of beer at the bar and
pushed through the crowded hall until he found a
rare vacant table. He took a long, satisfying
draught, wiped his lips and set to filling his pipe.
There was a card game playing adjacent and he
watched in half-interest as he concentrated on
getting an even light to his bowl.

The game wasn't going too well: two players
were arguing. Grimm ignored the high spirits and

scrutinized a painting of the pyramids above the bar. However, the contretemps nearby got more heated and then one of the men leapt up and hurled himself on to the other while he was still seated. The recipient's chair up-ended, playing cards scattered and the two men spilled over jarring Grimm's table so that his beer had gone before he could say a civilized adios to it. Grimm pulled out one of his irons and leaned over to the two men locked at his feet. Just as the attacker raised his fist to deliver a blow to the other's face, the barrel of Grimm's Smith and Wesson pressed into his throat.

'I came in here for a quiet drink, pal,' Grimm muttered, 'and I sure intend having one. OK?'

The man nodded as best he could with the weapon against his Adam's apple, stood up gingerly and backed off. The first man to fall had recovered and was getting to his feet with the intention of taking advantage of his opponent's sudden incapacity. With the speed of the professional he was, but without turning his head, Grimm pulled his other weapon and jabbed it at ninety degrees into the second man's stomach. 'That goes for you too, sunshine,' he said, still without looking at him.

The first man backed further and, when clear of the painful gun barrel, turned and scuttled towards the batwings. Grimm turned to the remaining combatant. 'I reckon there is justification in your grievance, pardner. Just continue your debate outside. OK?' The man was temporarily transfixed. 'Get him outa here,' Grimm said with such natural authority that two bystanders began to comply unquestioningly.

Seconds later the brawl could be heard continuing in the street and Grimm leathered his pistols. He stood up, shook his head as he surveyed the booze running to waste over his table, and crossed to the bar to reprovision.

'Thanks for what you did back there,' a voice said behind him as he bellied against the counter. It was a feminine voice, oozing sex. He turned. The voice belonged to an equally sexy body wrapped in a figure-hugging dress, bosoms exaggerated by up-lifting corsetry. Some folks said that older women shouldn't dress like that. Under the thick make-up, she sure was middle-aged as the signs testified: the beginnings of bags under the eyes, the turkey skin at the neck and between the up-thrust bosoms. But he was no chicken and that was sexy.

'Name's Sue Randall. But folks call me Suez Sue. I own the place.'

'Yeah, Suez,' he said, turning the word over in his mind. 'Saw the name outside. Suez. Where you get a name like that?'

'Can't rightly recall now.'

'You been out Egypt way?'

'No. Dunno how I got the label.' She drew on her cigarette, blew out the smoke and laughed. 'Of course, I always get some wise ass says it's on account of my big canal.'

Grimm remained mute. One of the old school, such talk from the lips of a female of the species kinda embarrassed him.

'But any guy talks like that sure don't get to see it!' she added.

Even more uncomfortable, Grimm dug one hand into his pocket in search of coins while he raised the other to get the barman's eye.

'No, no,' she said, clicking her fingers. 'You don't have to pay. You did me a good turn back there. Everything's on the house for you tonight.' She winked at him as the barman stopped serving someone else and began to move her way. 'And I mean *everything*, pardner,' she added. 'Now you have me at a disadvantage. You know my name, but I don't know yours.'

'Grimm, ma'am,' he said as the barman presented himself. 'Jonathan Grimm.'

'Right, Mr Grimm,' she said taking his arm. 'First, what can I tempt you with? Bourbon?'

'Sure.'

The barman listened, saw her nod, and left momentarily to return with two glasses and a top-dollar bottle in the other. She beckoned for Grimm to pour. He did the honours and pushed her glass towards her.

'And what do you do for employment, Mr Grimm?'

'Ain't in nobody's employ but my own, ma'am.'

'So, in what business do you engage?'

He sniffed the liquor before downing it. 'I sell things.'

'Ah, trade.' She appraised him while she took some of her own bourbon. 'I must say, Mr Grimm, you don't look like a merchant. Still, they do say that appearances can be deceptive.'

'They do that, ma'am.' He finished his drink and she refilled it. She saw she was to get nothing without prompting so she went on. 'How's business?'

'Win some, lose some. But I make three squares a day.'

She dropped her head and shook it as she

chuckled. 'Jeez, you must think me a nosy cow. But the reason I ask, it's plain as a boil on a hog's ass that you're right handy with that pistol. I hold admiration for a man who can handle his pistol.' She rolled her eyes. 'Anyways, I could sure do with a real man about the place. For protection, you understand. Things can get out of hand once in a while in an establishment like this.'

'Sorry, ma'am. Wish I could oblige, but I ain't in the market. But thanks for the offer.'

'Pity. Well, if you were to change your mind. ...' She refilled his glass again. 'Meantime, Mr Grimm, what is your pleasure? I got lots of girls to choose from. All trained to give the discerning man a good time. On the house, like I said. Tonight is your night.'

He tapped his glass. 'This is enough, ma'am.'

She looked at the ornate clock at the back of the bar. 'Time for me to make a circuit of the establishment. Just to show my face about the place. You sure I can't arrange anything? We cater for every taste.' She leant over to him and spoke quietly. 'What is it? You fancy a young man maybe? A boy? Little girls? Anything you like. They'll do anything you wish.'

Grimm was out of his depth. He shook his head weakly. 'You've been too kind already, ma'am. Leave the bottle. It's good stuff. I'll have a couple more slugs before I take my leave.'

'Well, don't forget to say goodbye before you go.' She began to move away. 'Thanks again.' Then she swirled towards the stairs, nodding to a patron here, somebody there.

Grimm looked around and spied a vacant table. He picked up the bottle and glass and crossed to it.

He sat alone for a spell, watching the drinking, carousing, card-playing. The air was getting thicker with smoke. Regularly some poke would stagger upstairs. A waiter passed and Grimm caught his arm as he returned.

'In a minute, sir,' the man said. 'I'm half-way through an order.'

'I ain't ordering, son. Just a question.'

'Yes, in a minute, sir.' The waiter made to move but his arm was transfixed by fingers, old but as unmoving as cast iron.

'I said I only have a question, son,' Grimm continued. 'These little girls upstairs.'

'You want one, sir? See Madam Suez.'

'No. How many you got up there? How old are they?'

The customer who had ordered drinks was shouting for attention but the transfixed waiter could see he wasn't going to get away until he had answered whatever the old-timer wanted to know. 'There's two. One's nine and the other's eleven. You wouldn't believe what they can handle.'

'Never mind the sales pitch. Where'd they come from?'

'I don't know that I am at liberty. ...' The cast-iron fingers gripped tighter.

'You're at liberty to get your head smacked,' Grimm hissed.

The waiter's pain-filled eyes looked one way, then the other. 'Madam has an arrangement with an establishment,' he explained in a low voice. 'They are supplied on a commercial basis.'

'Name names, friend.'

'Er. ...' The waiter faltered. The hurt in his arm was beginning to dominate his brain making thought difficult. 'Er … an orphanage. Forget the name.'

'Where?'

'Let me … think.' The waiter's eyes closed. 'Tucker's Gap.'

Grimm released the arm. The waiter would have won a prize in a fifty-yard dash with the speed that he shot away. At the bar Grimm exhaled one word. 'Jesus.' Then he exhaled another word before yanking up his picket pin and moving out. 'Shit.'

EIGHT

Leather creaked under him. What the hell had he let himself in for? Why in tarnation was he bothering his skull with the offspring of a scumbag owlhoot? Must be getting sentimental in his old age. Jeez, this was costing him money. He was already one bounty in arrears as a result of this escapade. That needed catching up on. What was more, it had been a bad year. There were other hides to get across his saddle. He'd got a roll of dodgers in his jacket. Yet, here was he, riding back into the middle of nowheres.

Outside the orphanage, he dismounted and, although stiff from riding, hitched his horse powerful quick at a stanchion and stepped up on to the verandah. He opened the door, thumping it as he passed into the entrance hall of the building. At the foot of the stairs he was met by Mrs McCarey. 'What the …?' was all she could get out.

He threw open the nearest door and was greeted by the sight of children seated at a table. His appearance elicited both surprise and anxiety amongst them, disturbed in their eating. But Sarah wasn't one of them.

'Where is she?' he asked.

'Mr Grimm,' the woman snapped. 'You are frightening the children.' She turned her head. 'Jack! Jack!'

Before Grimm could make any further investigations her husband appeared. 'What is going on here?'

'I've come for Sarah Toomey.'

Mr McCarey raised his hands. 'Mr Grimm, please, if you will, stay here.' He gestured to his wife. 'Elizabeth, go and fetch Sarah and we will sort this out.'

Grimm nodded. He could see and hear that the commotion was disturbing the kids. As Mrs McCarey went upstairs he refused a chair and stood, drumming his hands against his sides while the man stuck a finger down his stand-up collar. There were voices and then Mrs McCarey appeared at the stair's top. 'She doesn't want to come, Mr Grimm.'

'The hell she doesn't!' Grimm roared. He pushed past the man and bounded up the steps.

'Jack, do something,' Mrs McCarey shouted.

Grimm found Sarah's room. It was a small dormitory with half a dozen children and two grimy-looking beds. Sarah backed when she saw him. 'No. I don't want to go with you.'

He advanced, taking her hand and she tried to pull away from his grip. He grabbed her small face with his other hand and forced her to look at him. 'This is a bad place for you. I'm taking you away.'

'Where to?'

'Your ma's maybe. I don't know yet. But one thing's for sure, you ain't staying here. Now get your things.'

She shook her head. He picked her up by her waist and heavy-footed out of the room with his burden.

'This constitutes kidnapping,' Mr McCarey said when he got downstairs. 'A serious offence in this territory. She doesn't want to go with you. You are not a parent or legal guardian.'

'Kidnapping, huh!' Grimm growled, pointing a finger at the man. 'I want the gal's horse out front pronto. Fully rigged, just like she rode it in.' He swung the authoritative finger at the woman. 'And you get Sarah's clothes and such together in a bag.' Neither moved. 'Now, listen up, both of you. I found out a few things. All that's missing from this place is an addition to the sign. It should say Orphanage and Whorehouse Supply Service. The one reason I ain't seeing this place closed here and now is I ain't got the time to pick up the pieces. At the moment I only see myself having responsibility for one of the poor kids you got here. Now move!'

NINE

They rode for four days and Grimm was getting low on rations when he pulled in for the night. He was aiming for Lobo Wells which would put him on the trail for Yellowrock. He figured the town was close but it was too dark to go further and then have to face the matter of finding a place for the girl. He dismounted and tended to the animals. Just as he'd finished he caught her looking at him but she averted her gaze. In a way she was pretty but her face was pale. 'You get outside much, gal?'

'Yes, I play outside. Ma says I'm a tomboy.' She said the last bit quick as though she was used to saying it.

'Well, the sun doesn't put much colour in your cheeks, does it?'

'Ma says I don't tan.' She thought about it. 'Ladies use stuff from a box to put colour on their cheeks.'

'Not all of 'em. A gal needs some natural colour. Sign of being healthy. You shouldn't be that pale. What they been a-feeding yuh in that orphanage place?'

'Grits.'

He turned around slowly, quartering the

wilderness. 'Grits, eh? Seems like we could both do with some fresh meat inside us.' He pulled his rifle out of the saddle boot. 'Stay here, and don't make no noise. I'll see what I can rustle up.'

He walked into the brush, moving against the wind. He took big strides at first to put some distance between himself and the noisy horses. Eventually he came to a spot where the sage thinned. He scrutinized the earth and noted the sun-dried droppings of small animals. Promising sign. Likely a big-ears.

He glanced back to check the child hadn't followed him, then he lay down, staking out the clearing with the rifle cocked, his elbows on the ground. He shifted his body till it was comfortable; the operation needed stillness and patience. Age was bringing discomfort to his joints and he needed to fix himself into a congenial posture if he was to set still for a spell. For that reason he was real glad when a jack-rabbit loped into the clearing after a few minutes. The critter paused in full view, then seemed suspicious as he looked around; so Grimm pressed his cheek into the stock, aimed and fired.

The animal did a head-over-heels flip under the impact. The hunter hauled his body up and walked over to his prey. It was twitching, but only with a lifeless nervous spasm for it had been a clean kill. It was warm to his touch as he picked it up by its rangey back legs.

'Gather some kindling for a fire,' he called to the girl when he returned. 'We'll soon have ourselves a meal as good as any slick city restaurant.'

After they'd eaten their fill, he ensured she was cosily wrapped in her blanket. Relaxing before turning in himself, he lit up his pipe and took out his wallet to check his assets. The action was absent-minded and he returned the wallet to his pocket without much thought.

'Are you rich?' she unexpectedly asked from the other side of the fire.

'I thought you were asleep, young lady.'

'I saw you counting your money. Are you rich?'

'You shouldn't spy on folk like that. Besides, it ain't manners to ask somebody about their assets just out of plain nosiness.'

She looked at him with that ornery look he was getting used to which meant she wouldn't rest up with her fool questions until he'd given an answer.

'No, I ain't rich,' he said. 'Now git some shut-eye.'

They got into Lobo Wells the next morning. As he'd guessed it had only been a hoot and a holler with the result that the day was still young when he parked the horses in shade at the end of town. He had two pieces of business to settle in the place: get the girl out of his hair once and for all, then get pointed in the direction of Yellowrock and hit the trail. Of the two exercises he knew by experience the latter was going to be by far the easier.

'What are we going to do here, Mr Grimm?' Sarah wanted to know as he helped her down.

He wanted his young charge to be as presentable as possible when he made overtures to get her settled. He cast an eye over her. Any signs of her recent clean-up had disappeared somewheres along the trail. He glanced around and his ancient eyes could make out a BATHS sign way down the street.

'Well, first off, you gotta have a bath, young lady,' he said, taking her hand.

'Oh, not again. I've already had one this month.'

Her protestations didn't last and he was soon pushing open the door to the establishment. He was glad the place was in the care of a woman; made him feel more comfortable about handing the girl over. 'I'd be obliged if you could see that she gets the trail dust off, ma'am,' he said, dropping coins into the woman's hand.

Outside with only himself for company once again, he set off along the street, getting the layout of the place and locating the facilities. It wasn't long before one amenity in particular caught his eye: the saloon. Inside the smell was pleasantly beery and smoke-laden. Even the barman, a long unhappy-faced fellow, didn't put him off.

He bellied up to the bar and ordered a whiskey. Firing his pipe he soaked up the atmosphere. Toting the gal around he'd been missing out on relaxation, that was for sure. He took another couple of drinks while he savoured his pipe and appraised the clientele. The establishment was near full, the bulk of its users dressed like miners. Hardly a cowpoke in the place. And certainly nobody he could ask questions of on the matter of a place for Sarah.

But he still needed to have some idea of distances so he asked the sourpuss behind the bar and learned that Yellowrock was some forty miles north.

'Ain't no point in trying your luck there, stranger,' the barman added, digging a pinky into his ear and judiciously examining whatever he unearthed. 'The lode is thinning and the place is already crowded out with pokes scratching where there's nothing but useless rock. There's only trouble waiting for any new bozo goes pushing his nose in.'

'It's OK, pal,' Grimm said. 'I ain't in the gold game. But much obliged for the tip.'

He took a replenished glass to a table, but decided he wouldn't stay here long. Just enough time for Sarah to get cleaned up. He could read disappointment in the eyes of many drinkers. Many would have trekked west attracted by the promise of Eldorado, only to find the place sewed up. The big bonanzas with yellow metal for all comers were few and far between: Tombstone, California, the Yukon. Yellowrock would be like most sites, a flash in the pan, at best a few months profitable digging and panning for a lucky handful. Here, there was little money and loads of resentment.

'Where's the john?' he asked the barman after he'd emptied his glass.

The man thumbed the rear. 'Out back.'

Minutes later the bounty-hunter was stepping out of the lean-to where he'd emptied his bladder when something crashed down on the side of his head and he collapsed in the dust. He was dazed but aware enough to sense eager fingers exploring his pockets. He figured the scenario: in a drinking-parlour full of near destitute men he had flashed a gold eagle across the bar in payment for his drink.

Gathering his physical resources he lashed out with a heel and rolled. As he rose he could see he had badly caught the shin of one of his assailants.

'You're panhandling the wrong fella,' Grimm said, finally coming to his feet. 'That was the last of my cash.'

Suddenly his arms were transfixed, each held momentarily by two hands as inflexible as horse-hooves; held just long enough for his slicker to be raised and his guns to disappear.

'You bastard,' the limping man said, gripping his smarting shin. 'You're gonna pay for that.'

There were three and Grimm accepted there was an inevitability about the outcome of the forthcoming face-up. By intention he had never been a fist-fighter. His profession required leather clearance at speed and exact control of hair-triggers. That in turn required certain qualities in the hands: that they should be sinewy and delicate, features not associated with hands used as hammers. In the early days his body had had an accompanying agility which provided a compensating utility in physical face-ups, but that had long since been surrendered for the stiffness of age. Now he had but one remaining skill: the use of firearms. Take away the tools of his trade and he couldn't handle your average prairie waddy in a scrap.

A gloating anticipation in his eyes, the man squared up to him and swung. The Reaper managed to block the first punch on his arm, sidestepping so that he took the second on his shoulder. But they were jarring, numbing punches.

Oh well, in for a cent in for a dollar. He twisted his hips and lashed out with his boot as the man advanced further, catching his knee. As his surprised opponent went down, Grimm chopped at the back of his neck with the side of his palm, feeling the shock of the impact jarring up his ancient arm. He leapt on the fallen man's back and tried to immobilize him. His blows had been enough to temporarily daze the man, but that was all, for next, he himself was slung over into the dust with little effort.

He rose but the man was quick and sledged a fist into his belly. As Grimm crumpled forward the man crossed the other fist solidly into the bounty-hunter's jaw, curving him violently backwards so that his skull crashed against the ground. He rolled on to his front and crawled towards the back door of the saloon, sensing the big man towering over him.

Slowly he used the door-handle to haul himself to his feet. He turned. For his own dignity he had offered token resistance. Now there was nothing for it but to accept the inevitable. And it came: in the form of another set of iron knuckles to the face. He felt the projection of the door-handle painfully hard against his spine. Another rock-hard fist to the belly and he was down again. A boot repeatedly slammed into his ribs and the breath went out of him altogether. He tried to rise but his elbows gave way and he fell, awkwardly tangled amongst beer kegs.

He had no sense of time and didn't know how long he lay in that manner before hands grabbed him. Through the daze of pain he felt himself being hoisted and dragged. Interminably his knees scraped the ground as he was dragged further into the alley, then dumped. He tried to move, see where he was, but the damned boot came again. Seemingly he lost the capability of breathing through the massive ache left by the boot as it slammed again and again into what was left of his ribcage.

That was the last he remembered.

*   *   *

Vague, blurred light registered in his brain. Judas Priest, he owned a repository of pain rather than a body. 'No more,' he groaned. 'No more.'

He tried to curl away from the jabbing boot but he couldn't move his body. Jeez, he hoped to slip back into whatever void he had been lodged but consciousness frustratingly asserted itself. Then, a ceiling. What do you know, he wasn't in the alley. A clean smell. Freshness. A voice.

'You're all right.' It was a man's voice. 'Don't try to move. Don't even speak if it hurts.'

Eventually he could make out a face, benign, benevolent, one that didn't threaten to put the boot in. Words came out of the face. 'I'm Doctor Lander.'

'Where am I?'

'It's what goes for a hospital in Lobo Wells. Had to set it up when the casualties first started coming in from the camp. Cave-ins and such.'

'How did I get here?'

'You were lying beat up in an alley. Your daughter found you and had the presence of mind to summon me.'

'Daughter?' Grimm groaned.

'Yes, Sarah.' The doctor smoothed his shock of white hair that contrasted with a full black beard. 'The girl's a real credit to you, you know. If it hadn't been for her you would have stayed unattended to, and complications could have set in.'

'Complications? What's the damage, Doc?'

'Bruised ribs. Maybe one's cracked. I've strapped them up. Cut-up face. We've cleaned that up, seen it doesn't get infected. General all over bruising.'

'How long have I been like this?'

'One and a half days.'

'Jeez, so much lost time.'

'No, not lost time. Do not regret the period you have been asleep. It has been time well spent. There's a point in illness when sleep is the best cure.'

Grimm made to rise but fell back. 'Who did it? I didn't see the varmints.'

'Neither did anyone else. It's a common occurence these days. Pickings ain't too good out at Yellowrock these days so the town here's got more than its fair share of penniless would-be miners.'

'Where's the girl?'

'Outside. My wife called her when she saw you rousing.'

He heard Sarah's voice. Then he felt her soft hand touch his fingers.

'Thank you for what you did, Sarah,' Grimm said, trying to respond to her touch.

'Do you think you could manage to feed your father?' the doctor asked. 'I'll wager he's a mite hungry at this time. He should be able to take broth.'

What was with this 'father' business? Hell, he didn't feel like arguing. Resting, taking broth, yes.

TEN

'She ain't my daughter, Doc,' Grimm said when the doctor came to check him some time later. 'The kid's an orphan I picked up on the trail back a spell.'

'Odd,' the doctor observed. 'She definitely said that she's your daughter. I never questioned it once she'd told me.' He nodded to some colourful weeds in a jar on a table near the bed. 'Even picked some flowers for the invalid she did.'

Odd sure is, Grimm thought as he glanced at the sorry-looking specimens. Figured she hated me. She sure got reason to. Mind, her telling folks he was her father could be a good sign. If she was spinning that yarn then she hadn't told the doc about his killing her actual father. These were his musings but out loud he said, 'Don't tell her I've told you the truth. If that's the way she wants you to see it, ain't no reason to spoil her game. Where's she been while I been in dreamland?'

'Don't worry. My wife has been looking after her. Our own children have grown up and gone so she knows about kids.'

'The gal, she cotton to that arrangement, your missus looking after her?'

The doctor handed him a cool drink. 'Reckon so.'

Grimm swallowed the drink. 'Ain't made no attempt to run away or anything like that?'

'No,' the medical man chuckled. 'Why should she?'

'Ain't no figuring her,' Grimm said. 'That's the only sure thing I know about her.'

'What are your plans with regard to her?'

'Want to see her fixed up with someone.'

'Don't know whether that will be possible hereabouts. It's become a mite rough with the spill-over of no-goods from the camp. But she's OK with us until a permanent place can be found.'

Grimm heard some noises in the next room. 'That her?' he asked pointing in the direction of the door.

'No, sir. That's another patient. A mite worse off than you. Gunshot case. Bad, but he'll survive.' He stepped back and considered his patient's heavy lids. 'Now you get back to sleep. That was a sleeping draught I just gave you.'

When Grimm finally woke he was drowsy but didn't intend any further resting up. He had work to do. His chest was stiff and sore but no insurmountable handicap. He donned his pants and boots, then eased on his jacket. He checked the pockets: his pipe and tobacco, the spare shells he always kept in his breast pocket. He gathered the remainder of his gear and went outside into the corridor. He opened the door of the adjacent room and put his head inside. The patient of whom the doctor had spoken was lying on a bed with his back to the door. But he was awake and turned when he heard the door open. Grimm couldn't believe his eyes. 'Hammersley!' he said in surprise. 'Is that you?'

'Grimm,' the man chuckled weakly in recognition. 'I heard there was someone next door. Never figured it would be you, you old son-of-a-gun. How long you been getting involved in saloon brawls?'

'Wasn't exactly a brawl. Got jumped out back.' He winced slightly as he eased himself into a chair alongside the bed. 'What happened to you?'

'In the line of business. Tried to rope in a hard-case but his buddies got the drop on me. I took a couple of slugs. They left me for dead but I got picked up by a supply wagon and the fella brung me in.'

'It'll take more than a couple of slugs to punch your ticket.' Grimm became serious. 'The hard-case you were aiming to corral. Wouldn't be Von Hoffman, would it? Out at a mining camp called Yellowrock?'

Hammersley paused, then said, 'No use trying to fool you, Jonathan. You'd find out sometime anyhows. Yeah, it was Von Hoffman. You after him too?'

'You know darn well I would be.'

'How would I know that?'

'Because you dug up Toomey and took him in to Fort Smith for payment. You'd know it was me that put Toomey into the sod. And you'd have learned from the Fort Smith law office that his compadre was thought to be out here in Yellowrock.'

'You know the rule, Jonathan. It's the one who takes in the meat that gets paid for it.' He could see the visiting bounty-hunter wasn't impressed with the logic of his argument. 'Listen, we can strike a deal on Toomey.'

'You're darn tootin' we can,' Grimm said, rising. He took Hammersley's gun-belt from the bed-rail and threw it to the floor near the door. Then he started going through the pockets of the jacket draped over the chair until he found a purse-bag containing coins. He slackened the drawstring and emptied the contents in his hand. Small change. Next the pants, but he came up with nothing. Hammersley winced in pain as Grimm moved his head and raised the pillow. He picked up the revealed wallet and extracted the wad of bills. He dropped the empty wallet back on the bed. 'Settling accounts, Lee,' he said making for the door.

'Jeez, don't take all of it, Jonathan.'

Grimm ignored him and picked up the discarded gun-belt, draping it over his shoulder. In the corridor he closed the door and made his way to the surgery. He could hear sounds coming from inside so he knocked before entering. His knocking had been courteous but didn't save embarrassment. There was a half-naked female patient on a bed and what the doc was doing didn't look like it had come from a medical text-book. 'I forgot to lock the door,' the medic said in embarrassment to the woman as he got awkwardly to his feet.

'Sorry about the intrusion, Doc,' Grimm said, 'but I'm signing myself off the books.'

'I thought you'd still be asleep,' the doctor muttered, hastily fixing his pants. 'You won't say anything about this?'

The Reaper smiled slightly. 'As far as I'm concerned you're a good doc. You know your stuff.' He looked at the woman, now covered by a sheet. 'Mind, don't suppose I have to tell you that, ma'am.' He looked back at the doctor. 'How much do I owe?'

The doctor still looked flustered. 'Don't worry about that. It's on the house.'

Grimm shrugged. 'That's mighty kind. The guy next door, how long will he be laid up?'

'Another couple of days at least. He's lost some blood. Then there's the stitching to take out.'

'These are his guns,' Grimm said laying them on the surgery desk. 'Hide them away for a spell.' He opened the wallet. 'How much will his bill be including board?'

'Er, thirty dollars.'

Grimm counted out some bills. 'There's fifty.'

'He a friend of yours?'

'Kinda. But to be on the safe side make sure he don't get his hands on his guns till I'm outa town!' He counted out some more money. 'There's a hundred for you to look after the girl. I'm sure your good wife can get her fixed up someplace permanent in due course.'

'Of course.'

Grimm touched his hat. 'Sorry for the intrusion, ma'am. Hope you get better, whatever's ailing yuh.'

Outside he pondered on the situation. Now he knew for definite that Von Hoffman had been at Yellowrock, maybe still was. But Hammersley's débâcle meant the hard-case knew at least one bounty was aware of his where-at and how a stranger wearing a brace of six-guns just couldn't go riding in to the camp without expecting to meet trouble head-on.

He thought of Sarah. He had no qualms about leaving her with the doc and his missus. By all accounts the girl seemed to be happy there. What he had witnessed in the surgery didn't mean the doc was a pervert, just human.

ELEVEN

After Grimm had checked his horse was well stabled at the livery he moseyed around the town. Lobo Wells must have been an inoffensive-looking place before it had become burdened by the overspill of human dross from the mining camp. He casually paced the full length of the main street while he exercised his stiffened limbs and thought on the matter of getting to Yellowrock.

Near the end of the town stood a large building serving as the warehouse for EXCELSIOR SUPPLIES, the company named on the signboard over the double doors. Two men were talking as Grimm passed and he overheard their words.

'Mitchell ain't gonna be able to make it, boss,' a man in overalls was saying. He was leaning on the bed of a large four-team wagon on which he had just deposited some bags. 'In bed, sickening with a bad cold, his old lady says.'

'Shoot,' the other man said with a disdainful nose-in-the-air set to his face. Clad in a suit, he looked a boss-man. 'Ain't never knowed nobody for being sick so much. How long will it take you to load up?'

'Late afternoon should see it finished, Mr Whitworth.'

Grimm looked past the double doors. The mote-laden light from the transom fell on stacks of assorted bags and boxes. Business looked good.

'So we're aiming for a sun-up start,' the boss continued.

'I could do it myself, Mr Whitworth.'

'No, Cy. I can't afford to lose you for two days. There's more shipments coming in, need seeing to.'

'Well, finishing afternoon'll give me time to round-up somebody from the saloon. There's enough guys in there to choose from. They'll know the trail out to Yellowrock too.'

'All panhandlers looking for easy pickings, every mother's son of 'em. Wouldn't know the hay end of a hoss from its ass. No, ain't too keen on that, Cy. We need someone who can handle mules and looks trustworthy. A saloon bum stranger is jest as likely to light out with the load and sell it hisself somewheres.'

'Excuse me, gents,' Grimm said. 'Couldn't help overhearing. If you're looking for an extra hand, I'm looking for extra dollars.'

'Yeah,' the man called Whitworth said. 'I'm looking for a driver. Single return run out to Yellowrock. They've already had their main supplies but I got word there's still bits and pieces wanted out there. Anyways, who are you?'

'Grimm. Jonathan Grimm. At your service.' During his stay at the hospital he had been cleaned up and his clothes laundered so at least he looked a couple of pegs above a saloon bum.

'You driven a wagon before?'

'Ain't nothing about horses or what they pull I don't know about.'

'This ain't horses. Six-mule team.'

'Makes no never-mind. Like I say, anything leather will hold.'

'Grimm?' Whitworth chewed on the word. 'Name means nothing to me.'

'No reason why it should, Mr Whitworth. I ain't from Lobo Wells.' Grimm nodded down the street. 'But maybe Doc Lander would vouch for me.' He knew the doc couldn't say much on his behalf, but dropping the name sounded good.

'Ah, you know the doc. Good man. Plays one of the best hands of poker in town.'

'If you're worrying about me skedaddling with your supplies,' Grimm went on, 'I can leave collateral in the shape of my hoss and rig.' He looked wry. 'That is if I can trust you to look after her. Andalusian, a rare and expensive mount. I lay a lotta store on her. Saddle's a top-dollar rig too. Don't cotton to losing that either.'

'What do you normally do to earn your feed, Mr Grimm?'

'Businessman. Fell on hard times.'

Whitworth looked the man over while he thought further. There was something about the way the man carried himself indicating he was no stranger to the need of exerting his authority. And, a hint of education in the voice. Both characteristics gelled with the notion of a man who once had standing. As to whether he could trust him, that was a chance. 'Mr Grimm, if you're happy with ten bucks for two days' work, the job's yours.'

'Mr Whitworth, you've got yourself a driver.'

Come morning, Grimm was up early feeding and grooming his mare. After a little exercise out back he returned her to her stall. On the way to the stores building he could see the man called Cy swinging open the doors. Inside the wagon was already fully loaded and roped. Grimm placed his Winchester and a tarp bundle containing his pistols behind the seat. Innocuous wagon-drivers did not have sixguns strapped to their hips.

The wagon being too heavy for the two men to roll even the short distance out of the shed, the mules were brought to it from the corral. One by one they were harnessed in place. Grimm knew something of the art in setting up a team. The animals needed to be graded in weight, starting up front with the smallest as leaders. At the rear, the wheelers, the stockiest for the real hauling job. At the same time each pair had to be balanced so there was approximately equal strength in total down each side.

The animals in place, Grimm sat on the box and released the brake. Holding the bridles of the lead pair Cy led them forward so that the wagon came into the sunlight. They swung it parallel to the street and Grimm braked it. He dropped down and moved round the vehicle to test the connecting rod. He heaved on the wheels in turn to see how much give they had. While he was checking that the greasing was thorough he heard Whitworth's voice calling him to the office.

The boss gave him the manifest, listing flour, coffee and such, informing him that a guy by the name of Jess Henderson was acting as his agent out in Yellowrock. 'Well Mr Grimm,' he concluded. 'Just twenty miles of straight trail ahead due north. All that remains is for me to wish you safe passage.'

On the way back Grimm went into the stores

building and, from a pair of hooks, he fetched down a whip he had seen: ten-foot of rawhide on a packed stock. You didn't need to hit the animals but on a long trek you needed to extend your presence and that could only be done with a whip. He ran his fingers along the length, ensuring the hide wasn't cracked, then put it behind the box. Finally he walked round the animals checking the harness, then hauled himself up on to the box.

'We'll expect you back around sunset tomorrow,' Whitworth shouted. Grimm gestured up front to Cy acting as tender to release the bridles of the lead mules. The aged bounty-hunter shouted and cracked the whip. With that, the animals surged forward and the wheels began to roll.

TWELVE

It had been years since Grimm had had a six-team ahead of him. For the first few miles out of town he never let his concentration wane. The exact configuration of mules was probably new and the critters weren't quite sure what was expected of them, each acting somewhat as an individual. However, regular cracking of the whip close to one when he got uppity helped them to settle into the traces and eventually they were working as a team.

His chest was stiff and sore but not incapacitating. The dullness of the sky was the only fly in the ointment. The trail was new and rough. One thorough downpour and the co-operation he was getting from the mules could be strained to breaking point with nothing but thick hoof-gripping mud underfoot. In such circumstances a man on horseback could leave the trail and make reasonable headway over grass. But taking a six-mule wagon off the trail would be the action of a greenhorn.

He nooned by a creek with the first sight of foothills in the distance. He kept the animals in harness and watered each individually. He was just shaking out the dregs from the leathern bucket when he detected movement under the tarp. He put away the bucket and investigated the load. Hell's teeth, there was something moving under the covering. The manifest had said nothing about live freight. He went back to get his pistols but suddenly a recognizable flaxen head appeared.

'Sarah!' he mouthed. 'What the hell …?'

'I don't like it in here, Mr Grimm,' she said matter-of-factly.

'You ain't supposed to like it. Tarnation, you ain't supposed to be in there at all. Come on out.' He helped the girl disentangle herself and debouche. 'How and when did you get in there? And why?'

She ignored his questions. 'You were lighting out without me, weren't you?'

'Grown-ups have jobs to do, missy. Anyways, you had a nice place back there. They were treating you all right, weren't they?'

'Yes.'

'Then what was wrong with it?'

'The lady kept shouting at the man.'

Grimm remembered the doc's extra-mural capers and figured his missus had caught him giving out some of his unorthodox treatment. He exhaled noisily in frustration. Grimm led a life of decisions and action, and it was rare for him not to know what to do next. But he was sure nonplussed as of this moment. He didn't cotton to riding all the way back to Lobo Wells. If he did, there'd be the hassle of finding yet another place for the little monster that wore a frock.

'You stretch my patience, little woman. That you do.'

She smiled sweetly. Jeez, he knew her demeanour was false but didn't know how to handle it. Hardcases, lawmen, guys on the prod, he could handle. But forty pounds of feminine guile? Judas Priest.

'Get up on that seat,' he said in resignation.

When she was securely in place, he joined her, flicked the reins and they began to move. They had been riding a long time when they came to a pass cutting into the hills, the entrance of which was marked by a shock of fir and small pine. Grimm nudged the team slightly off the trail towards some healthy sward where they could graze, then halted the wagon in the shade of the trees to rest a spell and take bearings. Sarah's attention was attracted to the sound of squirrels chattering in the pines and she dismounted, running across to investigate.

Grimm shook his head with a smile of exasperation but refrained from reprimanding her yet again. It had taken him some time to learn that she was just a young kid after all and there is a limit to how much an oldster can cuss. He was also learning to see the world through a child's eyes. Down to brass tacks, what was more interesting than a family of noisy squirrels for God's sake?

He watched her a spell then looked upwards. The sky was still dull but the late afternoon was warm. When he had dismounted and ground-hitched the animals he stuffed his pipe and scratched a match. With the mules' heads deep in their nose-bags and Sarah occupied, he ran his hard glance over the terrain, up the tilting valley floor. Long-tailed jays flitted overhead. He shaded his eyes and looked to the hills, the ridges.

Wait. He squinted. There were riders, way up the pass. It was too far for his ancient eyes to make any positive identification but their legs were hanging low. That meant no saddles, and no saddles meant

Indians.

He let off the brake, took the bridle of the lead mules and eased them out of sight behind the trees. 'Sarah,' he said loudly, but not shouting. 'Keep within cover of the trees and stay close. There are Indians ahead.'

He kept his eyes on the redmen, remaining still until it became clear the redskins were headed their way. Indians did not necessarily mean trouble. But he wasn't going to chance it. 'Get up here with me, gal,' he said. 'We're moving.'

She did as she was bid and he swung further offtrail, angling to their right up a flanking boulder-studded slope. 'Keep your head down,' he ordered. 'There's a good gal.'

He kept a look-out as they rolled, occasionally catching glimpses of the redskin party making their way down the rocky downtaper of the pass end. There was no sign from them that the wagon had been seen. Topping the hogback ridge, he glanced back once more before the wagon lurched in its descent but the riders were now lost themselves beyond a screen of young fir.

The terrain was giving way to hilly meadows of rippled grass with foothills rising gently to their left. A chicken-hawk spiralled against the steel-blue sky as he glanced at the sun to keep track of their direction. 'We can slow down now, Sarah. We haven't been seen.'

'Would they have hurt us, Mr Grimm?'

'You never can tell, Sarah. But it pays to play safe.'

As they rolled he pondered on the incident and it made him think more of the welfare of the little girl. Out in the wilderness they could run into any kind of trouble. Indians, renegades. He could handle himself, but what if anything happened to him? Sarah needed to look after herself. And that meant handling a gun.

'Sarah,' he said after a spell. 'First chance we get, I'm gonna teach you how to use a gun. Just in case.'

'No,' she said adamantly. 'Guns are bad things.'

'Suit yourself.'

Later the terrain levelled out and he nursed the mules for a spell so they would not be too strained when it came to making the climb he could make out some way ahead. Under threatening clouds he twisted in his seat to scan the distant surroundings, first to the left then to the right. He was about to straighten up again when his attention was caught by a flicker of movement. At about four o'clock from his position were trees and it had seemed to him that it could have been a rider spurring forward to be out of sight when he had turned. He continued to stare but saw nothing more. Was it one of the Indians? He figured not.

Over the next rise he saw a shack way to the east. Not shy of necessaries he gave it no more thought. Detours would be wasteful with the animals making such heavy going of the terrain. As he angled the animals leftwards in the hope of cutting the trail again, he heard the distant rumble of thunder.

Ten minutes later and the heavens opened. Judas Priest. He leaned his weight on the brake and pulled hard on the lines. By the time he had got Sarah under the tarp she was soaked. Worse, the water was coming down cold. A bad sign with night drawing. Such conditions played hell with his rheumatism but they were accepted as part-and-parcel of the game. But the girl? She was shivering already.

'We're gonna try and make that shack,' he said. 'We need solid cover and a fire.'

THIRTEEN

With heads bowed the mules strained to haul their load through the deepening quagmire. It was good they made the shack when they did because much more headway would have been impossible for the stove-up critters. A man stood in the light of the opened doorway as Grimm pulled on the reins and heaved on the brake.

'Get your bodies inside,' the man shouted, foregoing any introductions, his voice raised above the rain. 'Ain't fit for a coyhoot out there.' The two travellers dropped down and scrambled for the welcome shelter.

'Settlers?' the man prompted once the weather was behind a closed door and Sarah was standing before a heartening fire.

'No,' Grimm said. 'Riding freight to Yellowrock.'

'Freight? Out of Lobo Wells?'

As he took off his hat and wiped the surplus water from his brow, Grimm appraised the room then the man. There was a black jacket and hat hanging from a hook, and the fellow wore trousers of the same colour putting Grimm in mind of his being a Quaker or something. He was around late thirties in years with tired, red-rimmed eyes set in a face that said that life was a handful for him.

'Yeah,' Grimm confirmed. 'Supplies from Lobo Wells.'

'I thought Whitworth had made that run his contract? Been taking supplies out there since the first strike.'

'Yeah, it's his wagon. His regular driver couldn't make it.'

'Well, you musta got lost. You're a way off the regular trail.'

'Saw a bunch of redskins on the trail aways back,' Grimm explained. 'They were ahead so I pulled off the trail and cut across country.'

The man's haggard features broke into a faint smile. 'You caused yourself unnecessary trouble, stranger,' he said. 'Indians ain't no bother in these parts.'

Grimm shrugged. 'Now I know.'

'Well, ain't no gain-saying you're welcome to stay over the night.'

'That's mighty kind, mister. You got cover for the team?'

'Yeah, a couple of lean-tos. Should just about be able to accommodate them.' He passed a towel to Sarah and, after rooting about in another room, he found a shirt and pants for her. Then he pulled on a slicker and, leaving the girl to dry off and don the clothes, the two men set about unharnessing the draught animals and getting them under cover. When they returned Grimm was carrying his Winchester and the tarp bundle containing his sixguns.

The man watched with unvoiced disapprobation as the bounty-hunter unwrapped the weapons and checked they hadn't got damp. 'I suppose a wagon driver needs armaments,' he said as he picked up one of the oil lamps and indicated for Grimm to accompany him into a back room. Grimm draped the gunbelt over the back of a chair and followed him. In the dim light of the back room the man went through the drawers of a cupboard, eventually extracting a set of clothes. 'Should tide you over till your own duds are dry,' he said.

Minutes later Sarah broke into laughter when her companion returned to the front room. Belonging to their host, the sleeves of the shirt finished half way down Grimm's forearms while the pants legs exposed almost a foot of his shins.

'Don't be sassy,' he grunted. 'And don't mock your elders, missy.'

'Sorry about that, fella,' the man said, hiding his own grin behind a hand. 'I ain't exactly your build.' Still smiling, he put a pot on the stove and stirred its contents. 'Stew,' he added, as he set the lid on the vessel. 'Left-overs. But there's ample for another two good meals. Sit yourself down.'

'That's mighty kind,' Grimm said, settling his aching bones on a chair by the fire. He looked at Sarah who had finally stopped giggling. He grinned and pointed. 'Look who's talking, missy.' The clothes she had been given weren't adult-size but they were still a mite too big for her and her hands were out of sight. 'Come here, scamp,' he chuckled. She did so and he helped her to roll up the sleeves and the pants bottoms.

'I was forgetting my manners,' the man said, turning from the stove. 'Name's Stanhope. Jim Stanhope.'

'Jonathan Grimm. Glad to make your acquaintance. The lass is Sarah. A niece of sorts.' He caught a look in her eye, maybe of some kind of satisfaction, as he voiced the white lie.

After the meal they were seated around the fire while Stanhope discussed the state of his livestock and crops. The rain against the roof had slackened and Grimm heard the noise of movement in another part of the shack. Sounded like it was coming from behind a door that hadn't been opened since their arrival. When the noise became the distinct sound of feet on boards he dropped his hand so that it was near the handle of one of his guns.

The knob turned and the door opened to reveal a woman, maybe a mite younger than Stanhope but with the same haggard look as the homesteader.

'This is Jonathan Grimm and his niece Sarah,' the man said, standing and making way for her. 'They got caught in the storm.'

'I heard voices,' she said.

'My wife Hester,' Stanhope said.

'Pleased to meet you, ma'am,' Grimm said, rising while she took a seat.

'Could you manage a little more to eat?' Stanhope asked his wife. 'You must try.'

'No.'

'Did you get some sleep?'

'Oh yes, eventually.' She enquired of Grimm his circumstances and the earlier conversation was repeated.

'You mind if I smoke, ma'am?' Grimm asked.

'No, of course not. You go ahead while I sort out some linen for you and the little girl.'

'I can do that, dear,' Stanhope offered. 'You stay by the fire.'

'No,' the woman said, rising. 'I need to occupy myself.'

FOURTEEN

Over breakfast the next morning Stanhope explained the best course for picking up the trail. The travellers took their leave and headed out. Once the team had settled, Grimm mused on the couple they had left behind them. The Stanhopes seemed real unhappy; so unhappy in fact he just couldn't understand why they stayed on at their little plot at the back of nowhere. There was something about their circumstances that didn't set right. But he had his own troubles without taking on board those of others.

And those troubles were added to when, an hour out from the shack, he heard a crunch behind him and the rear of the wagon lurched crazily. He whoaed the mules and heaved on the brake, casting his gaze back. A rear wheel was shattered, having finally given in to the relentless punishment of the rough terrain. The matter could be put to rights, there was a spare wheel suspended underneath the wagon, but it was a matter of time and energy. For a start the vehicle would have to be unloaded.

He and Sarah set to, lifting off the freight until there was a scatteration of containers around the wagon. Then, with his back to the side panel and straining his aged muscles, he gradually raised the unsupported corner, resting each time Sarah managed to slide in another freight bag to relieve him of the weight. It was a couple of hours before they were on their way again.

As Sarah had said, this was like an adventure. Huh.

Then, even before they made the regular trail again, another trouble revealed itself: he began sighting a lone rider. The guy could easily have caught them up but for some reason he was keeping his distance. It was plain he was dogging them. Chances were it was the same one who had been dogging them the previous day.

They should have made Yellowrock later that day but their digression coupled with the rough terrain away from the trail and the mishap with the wheel had set them back, so that by late afternoon according to his reckoning they were still some miles shy of the mining camp. Cursing, he decided to pull in for the night rather than attempt to make their destination in the dark. Sighting a hollow sheltered by trees he swung the wagon off the trail.

After he had lit a fire for warmth he could plainly see Sarah was tired so, rather than wait for cooked food they took a bite to eat from their store. They had coffee and he let Sarah close her eyes. Once she was asleep he made a furtive circuit of the site, looking and listening in vain for any intruders.

Then he walked through the trees some twenty yards until he found a natural curve against the bole of a tree. He returned to the camp-site. 'You don't have to wake, Sarah,' he whispered, getting a grip of the sleeping child and picking her up. 'I'm just moving you to another sleeping place. That's all.' She murmured without meaning, her eyes still closed and her body limp in his arms. He didn't want to alarm her by telling her they were likely to get an uninvited caller so he was grateful she didn't wake. She was only a slight figure but became a considerable burden for his ancient limbs as he picked his way through the darkness. He laid her against the tree between the exposed roots and snuggled the blanket around her. Oblivious to her changed circumstances she rearranged her body to fit the new position. He looked at her for a few seconds then returned once more to the camp. He used bags from the wagon to make two blanket covered dummies, then withdrew into the trees.

It was a full fifteen minutes before anything happened. Then he heard the man before he saw him. The crunch of twigs underfoot gave direction so Grimm knew where to look. Another minute passed and he saw a figure in the gloom on the opposite side of the clearing. As the man moved from the shadows for a second, something in his hand reflected firelight for a brief second. He held a pistol. Grimm wanted to learn more before he took any action: like what was the man's intention, and whether he had companions. The way he circled the glade suggested he was alone but Grimm still couldn't be sure there weren't others within hearing. Whatever he did would have to be noiseless.

Slowly the man worked his way in Grimm's direction. Grimm was perplexed. The man had traversed three quarters of the circumference of the clearing, doing nothing but watching. By this time he could easily have shot what he would have thought to be the sleeping figures. Or sneaked up and made his challenge. Either he was some strange fellow, or he was reconnoitering for someone else. Whatever the interloper's intention he was getting extremely close to the man who in turn was watching him. Unable to move out of the man's way without himself disturbing vegetation underfoot, Grimm would have to take some action. As the man passed him mere feet away he took it.

His pistol butt caught the man somewhere on the back of the head and the stranger dropped with a grunt, crunching vegetation in his fall. Grimm held his gun in the firing position but it was unnecessary as the man remained immobile and silent. The Reaper exhaled in irritation. The last thing he'd wanted to do was incapacitate the fellow until he'd found out what the hell was going on. He sheathed his weapon, bent down and hauled him towards the fire. The intruder was young, maybe twenty, and it was clear by the slackness of his form that he would pose no more of a threat for the time being.

Grimm groped round the wagon until he found some rope, then bound the inert figure. Ensuring the binding was secure he began shaking the man's shoulders. Eventually the man groaned and his eyes flickered open. 'What the hell happened?'

'Sneaking round somebody's camp earned yourself a pistol-whipping, stranger.'

The man groaned again.

'You got friends close?' Grimm asked.

'Yeah,' the man murmured after a pause, 'but not close.' The words were slurred and Grimm could tell the guy was having trouble trying to herd his wits into the corral.

'Well, you can tell me all about it after I've had a look at that skull of yours.' The examination revealed a sizable lump. 'You'll live,' Grimm concluded. 'Now what's this all about, fella, dogging us and snooping round our camp?'

'I'm with a posse riding out of Lobo Wells. Under Marshal Jones.'

'What's your name?'

'Clay Holser.'

'What's a posse doing out in the wilds at this time of night?'

Following his concussion the man was still having trouble gathering his thoughts and he waited a spell before continuing. 'Road agents have been knocking over supply wagons to the mining camp. We've been trailing you on the look-out for them. But then you went and left the trail and made it difficult for us to keep track of you.'

'That sounds like I was set-up as a decoy?'

'Not really. It was a regular run. And you volunteered.'

'It would have been easier to explain the situation to me before letting me ride out.'

'Marshal reckoned you might not have gone through with it.'

'Well, Mr Clay Holser, I don't cotton to being put in jeopardy without being told.' Grimm appraised his captive. The man didn't look well. 'Get some sleep,' he went on. 'We'll sort this out in the morning.'

FIFTEEN

Grimm was awake before dawn. By the time he had watered and harnessed the mules the first rays of the sun were bouncing off the clouds and lighting up the hollow.

'Freshen up and have a bite to eat,' he said to Sarah as she woke but she was too interested in their new companion. 'We had a visitor during the night,' Grimm told her in answer to her questions. He spoke to the man but he didn't respond. He shook him, gently at first then more vigorously but couldn't get any reaction other than a subconscious grunt. He'd hit the man harder than he imagined. If that was the case it had been bad policy for the man to sleep. Too late now.

'Why doesn't he wake?' Sarah asked.

'Reckon he's in a bad way,' Grimm grunted. Looked like nothing was going right on this caper. The girl was a jinx. He looked at the strengthening light coming through the trees. He could, of course, resume the journey but he felt some responsibility for the lawman's condition, even though the critter had brought it upon himself by sneaking around the way he had. Bouncing about on the back of the wagon might not be the best thing for him.

'Ain't gonna be any good for him to travel further,' he admitted. 'He'll have to be tended to and rest up in comfort. For his sake I don't think we should chance them having any amenities at the camp.' Stuck with a wounded man who needed attention, the only place he could think of was the Stanhopes. He loosed off an expletive in a tone low enough not to be heard by Sarah then concluded in an audible voice, 'There ain't no way of avoiding it. We're gonna have to go back to the shack.'

He rearranged the load to make a flat surface then hauled the man up on to the wagon and secured him. He got their things together then indicated for Sarah to get aboard. He climbed up into the driver's seat alongside her and urged the mules into a semi-circle to head them back whence they had come.

Stanhope was working his vegetable patch when the wagon rolled up for a second time. He rammed his shovel into the soil and made his way to the shack to greet his visitors. Hester relinquished her washing chores and came to the door, her hands and forearms lathered pink. Grimm explained the circumstances to the couple and the two men manoeuvered the injured man into the shack. The woman supervised his laying on a bed then fetched a basin of water and cloth.

'Can the girl stay here while I continue to Yellowrock?' Grimm asked Stanhope as his wife began to bathe the lawman's head. 'I can't take her now I know the wagon is likely to be attacked. She'd only be on your hands a short spell. I figure it won't be long before the marshal arrives looking for his deputy.'

He hadn't realized Sarah was listening. 'I ain't

staying,' she said before the man could answer. 'I'm coming with you.'

'Goddamn it, gal,' Grimm exclaimed. Then he forced a pleasant tone into his voice. 'See sense, kid. There's gonna be trouble out there. The young lawman says there are road agents after the freight.' He didn't explain his true mission of going after Von Hoffman. That was another reason why he didn't want the girl along.

'Come, child,' Hester said to Sarah. 'You can help me. We need to tend to the sick man. You can help me cook. And we can do jobs about the house together.'

Sarah's face screwed up at the prospect. 'No.' Her voice showed obduracy. 'I'll run away.'

Stanhope looked at Grimm and the latter muttered, 'She means it.' Grimm rubbed his temple. 'Judas Priest, has that gal got a doggone mind of her own! Don't act like no kid should.'

'You just want to get shed of me,' Sarah went on.

That was true but it would make matters worse if he agreed.

'Well,' the woman said. 'We have to face facts. We can't keep the girl if she doesn't want to stay. I'd have no peace of mind if she ran off. It's wild country out here.'

'How far's Yellowrock on horseback?' Grimm asked Stanhope.

'A good horse would do it in a couple of hours.'

The bounty-hunter pondered on the matter then crouched down to the child's level when he came up with an idea. 'Listen, Sarah. Will you stay with these good people if I leave the wagon here?' He looked up at Stanhope. 'I could ride out and tell Whitworth's man in Yellowrock his wagon is here and he can arrange to fetch it. We'd cover it over so it wouldn't be spotted by any passing folk.'

Stanhope nodded in agreement.

'See,' Grimm said to Sarah, his eyes still at the child's level, 'leaving the wagon will mean I'll be coming back, don't it?' It didn't mean that of necessity but it sounded as though it had a logic. If it gave him a way of leaving the girl behind while he took on Von Hoffman, he didn't mind giving up his cover of being a harmless wagon-driver. He'd ridden into worse situations before with nothing but a slicker and his sixguns.

'That sounds reasonable,' the woman urged, looking at Sarah. 'And it means you'll be out of harm's way should your uncle meet up with any trouble.'

Grimm looked at the girl's eyes and could see she was about to blurt out that he wasn't her uncle; but for her own goddamn reasons she didn't.

'I tell you what,' Stanhope suggested. 'I can make you a doll. I got a suitable piece of wood amongst the lumber. You'd like that, wouldn't you?'

'And you and I can make a dress for it,' the woman added. 'All pretty like she's going to a dance.'

Sarah looked at her ancient companion. 'Promise you'll come back?'

'Promise,' Grimm conceded, trying to affect genuineness without betraying relief.

SIXTEEN

It was plain Stanhope's horse was a Sunday mount. Grimm couldn't have expected more. The man was a farmer and only used the sorrel for riding around his fields and for the occasional errand into town. But it was fresh and Grimm managed to get some pace out of it.

Sarah didn't know it but she'd seen him for the last time. Granted, when she wasn't being a pain in the ass she was a good kid. But in his trade he couldn't be encumbered. By his figuring he'd done right by her. At least he hadn't dumped her to fend for herself. The Stanhopes could get her to Lobo Wells and folks there would see that she got settled properly. Nor was he concerned what happened to Whitworth's wagon. Not for ten dollars he wasn't. Whitworth and the marshal had had no qualms about allowing him to volunteer unknowingly as a decoy. Whitworth could stew. No, the Reaper had got one aim now: to get Van Hoffman in tow, or his hide over a saddle, which way didn't matter. Then he would pick up his Andalusian in Lobo Wells, leave Stanhope's nag at the livery in town and head out for the nearest federal law office to claim the bounty.

The sorrel began to tire and he slacked up on the reins. There was no percentage in running the horse into the ground. After an hour he rested it up a spell. While he munched on some of Mrs Stanhope's biscuits he tried to recall Hoffman's features. He might need to identify the owlhoot pretty fast when he got to Yellowrock. But once more he cursed that he had lost his papers in the river way back.

He checked his guns and mounted up, resuming his journey real slow. Although he took to nursing the brute along, he noticed it was breaking stride with increasing frequency.

He'd just come out of mesquite and dropped into a gully when the horse faltered in stride. He was about to rein in when the sorrel's head went down. The creature's legs folded and Grimm toppled from the saddle. The fall didn't do his injured chest much good and he lay still for a few seconds grunting with the pain. The sorrel was better off than he, quickly back on its hooves with an apologetic look in its eyes to boot. Grimm stood up, rubbing his jolted shoulder. 'Ain't your fault, pal. You ain't used to this. Don't worry, I won't push you so hard.'

But he was wrong. When he noticed the animal was keeping its weight off one hoof he knew he wouldn't be able to push the brute at all. He bent down and felt the lower leg. 'Ain't broke, fella, but you ain't gonna be able to take a rider for a spell,' he muttered.

'Don't matter 'cos you ain't going no place.'

At the sound of the shouted voice, the Reaper's guns came out in the same instant that he became erect. Barrels aimed at ninety degrees from each other, he whirled round.

'You don't look a fool,' the raised voice went on.
'So don't use them pieces.' The advice was sound;
he would have been a fool to use them. There were
five rifles aimed at him from the gully's rim and he
was completely without cover. 'Drop 'em before
you git yourself blasted to hell,' the voice
continued. Grimm let the guns fall to the ground
and raised his hands.

While three men remained at the higher vantage
point with their rifles aimed at the loner, two men
clattered down the scree.

The first man to approach had a baby face
surrounded by a ring of ginger hair consisting of a
headful of unruly hair and terminating in a wispy
beard. 'What you doing out this way?' he wanted to
know, wielding the muzzle of a Sharps.

Grimm took the challenge coolly. 'Heading out
to Yellowrock.'

'You're out of luck, fella,' the second said. He
had a long nose that had a history of getting in the
way judging by the legacy of crookedness along its
length. 'They don't welcome any new diggers out at
Yellowrock.'

'He ain't no digger,' the ginger-haired one said.
'Not with those guns. And those hands ain't never
picked up a shovel neither.'

'Well, I'll be,' the other said. 'You know, Casey,
he looks like the jazzbo who volunteered to drive
Whitworth's wagon.'

'Is that so?' Casey muttered.

Grimm figured in the circumstances it would be
better if he kept up his cover. 'Yeah.'

'Huh,' Casey grunted. 'We been waiting for that
damn thing for over a day. What you done with it?'

So that was it. These no-goods were the

bushwhackers the deputy had talked of. 'Where the hell is it?' the man called Casey went on. 'Ain't knocked it over yourself, have yuh?'

'I had to leave it a-ways back. Wheel broke. Figured it was best if I rode on to Yellowrock to tell Whitworth's agent its whereat.'

Broken-Nose waved for his confederate still up on the gully rim. 'Come on down, Dwight.' The man addressed revealed himself and raised his rifle in acknowledgement. Grimm heard him shout an order to the two men at his side to fetch the horses and he watched him begin the descent. With the barrel shape of an indulgent man, he was older than his compadres and had some difficulty in negotiating the slope.

When he'd made the bottom, the one called Casey explained their findings to the older man who was plainly their leader.

'Well, you can tell us where the wagon is, fella,' Dwight said after he'd absorbed the information. His left eye closed when he spoke as though it was blind; but when he finished speaking it opened and there was definitely a functioning eyeball in it. The eye closed again as he added, 'Do us more good than Whitworth, won't it, boys?'

The others laughed. Grimm eyed the guns. 'I ain't no hero. And I don't owe Whitworth nothing. I don't mind showing yuh.' Needing to play for time while he figured how best to handle these bozos, he looked at the sun just falling below the gully's rim. 'But it's back quite a spell and I'm a stranger in these parts. I'm likely to get lost in the dark before I find the damn thing again. That's how I got lost in the first place.'

'Makes sense,' the oldster said, glancing along

the gully. There was a sheltered spot a hundred yards on. 'OK, we'll camp over there till morning.'

The muzzle of a gun nudged Grimm and he moved forward. At the proposed camp-site they were joined by the men leading the horses.

'Lenny,' the leader said as he appraised the place that would be their overnight home. 'When you've tethered the horses, hog-tie this varmint.'

Lenny was another youngster, his black hair meticulously parted down the middle so that it cascaded down both sides of his head.

'What they call you?' he asked of Grimm as he unfastened a length of rope from a saddle.

'Name's Morgan,' the bounty-hunter said.

'OK, Mr Morgan,' Lenny said. 'Let's have your wrists.' The young man's face and hands were loaded with puppy fat and there was a giggle in his voice as he spoke as though he didn't want to offend anybody.

Grimm allowed himself to be tied as Lenny built a fire and Broken-Nose rummaged through his saddle-bags. When the tying up was completed the others went about their business leaving one to keep watch on the prisoner allowing him no chance for making a break. Nevertheless he had a chance to think. There was no way he was leading this bunch of no-goods back to the Stanhopes. He'd got Sarah off his back all right, but he wasn't putting her in jeopardy again. Then he remembered the spare cartridges he always kept in his breast pocket. The hardcases had stripped him of his guns and searched him but had overlooked his breast pocket. The cartridges he kept there were the only advantage he had over them.

He looked at the fire. It was glowing hot. It was

an old trick but it could work again. But not yet awhiles. There were two questions: how and when?

Beans were heated in a pan and he was allowed to share them, an exercise for which his hands were temporarily freed.

Later they were staring quietly into the fire, coffee mugs in their hands.

'I'm itching for a woman,' Casey said, groping at his groin in a movement that Grimm had not seen previously outside of a menagerie cage.

'Waal, don't look at me, pal,' Broken-Nose said, moving away from the restless youngster.

'Jes' wait until we've sold the supplies from offa the wagon,' Dwight said. 'Then with the loot you can buy whatever you want.'

'I can buy what I want now,' Casey said. 'I ain't skint. Go on, boss. Let me ride out for a spell. Ain't nothing here to keep me till tomorrow.'

'We can make Yellowrock in an hour,' another said. 'Enjoy ourselves, spend the night there and be back for sun-up.'

A third supported the suggestion.

'OK, OK, get the hell out of here,' Dwight capitulated after a tense silence. 'But you be back at sun-up like you says or you'll have used them balls for the last time 'cos I'll shoot 'em off. Now git, you horny toad.'

Grimm watched the three saddle up and head out into the darkness. Three down, two to go.

'That's what comes of riding with kids,' Dwight said into the fire when the sound of their hoofbeats had finally died down on the night wind.

Grimm waited a spell in the silence then said, 'Nature calls.'

'Do it where you are,' Dwight said absently. 'We

ain't particular.'

'If you say so,' Grimm said, 'but what I got to unload you mayn't want nearby through the night.'

'Jeez,' the boss said. 'OK. Lenny, untie his feet and rope one ankle. Then take him out a few yards. But keep your gun on him. Just blast first and ask questions afterwards, he tries anything.'

Lenny jerked his gun. Grimm walked into the darkness with his rope shackle and did what he wanted to do.

When he got back to the camp-fire Dwight was sitting on his saddle blanket, eyelids drooping. 'Watch him,' he said as he lay down. Minutes later Grimm could hear his breathing becoming regular. One down, one to go. He thought again of the cartridges and looked at the fire. Conditions were right and he had to act fast because any second Lenny would be tying up his hands for the night. The problem was going to be how to get the bullets into the embers. Without surprise the operation would be ineffective so he needed to get them all well and truly into the fire.

'You any objection to me taking a smoke?' he grunted, like it was a last request. 'You know, afore we turn in.'

Lenny made a dismissive gesture. 'Why not? I ain't tired.'

Grimm fished out his pipe and tobacco pouch and filled the bowl. He deliberately ensured the activity was conducted in a slow and boring fashion so that when his hand eventually went to his breast pocket to return the pouch, the guard didn't notice that the fingers disappeared from view for an inordinate amount of time. Making sure that he had all the cartridges in his grip and they were well masked by his fist he withdrew his hand.

'OK for me to light up?' he asked, nodding towards the fire.

'Ain't no point in filling up your pipe if you ain't gonna smoke it, fella,' Lenny grunted.

Grimm nodded and looked around for a twig. As he picked up a suitable taper and poked it in the fire till it caught alight, he realized his actions were being closely watched. He held the flame over the bowl and hollowed his cheeks, drawing repeatedly until comforting smoke appeared.

'How long you guys been riding together?' he asked. As he spoke he lobbed the smouldering twig into the darkness away from the camp. For a moment the man's eyes followed the trajectory of the red glowing point. Only for a second, but enough for Grimm to lean over the fire and drop the cartridges.

'Ain't nothing to do with you, pal,' the man grunted. 'Now set yourself down again where I can see yuh.' The pistol pointed unwaveringly at Grimm's chest. 'And don't make it too long 'cos I'm gonna have to tie you up again.'

Grimm shrugged. Not knowing how long it would take for the missiles to ignite and not wishing to be a victim of his own ruse, he stepped back, trying to mask his movement by pretending to concentrate on drawing in smoke. He turned his back to the fire and casually took a few more steps away to the limits of the rope tethering his ankle. The outcome of the explosions would be unpredictable but if he was going to be on the receiving end of anything out of the fire, he preferred he got it in the back rather than the face.

He didn't have to wait long. Even though he was

expecting it, the first explosion jarred his nerves. But the effect on Lenny was catastrophic. An ember struck his cheek. He went rigid, eyes wide, his gun muzzle jerking in random directions as he clawed at his face. After the fragmented second it took Grimm to compose himself he leapt at his guard, wrenching the gun from his hand. Further embers from the fire scattered in a ten-foot radius as the other cartridges exploded in quick succession and the confused man made to run. Grimm caught him on the back of his skull with the pistol so that he collapsed face down.

Aroused from his slumber the elder man, equally confused, was fighting to get out of a blanket roll peppered with glowing holes. Freeing himself, he scrabbled for his holster. Grimm spun and fired. His victim shouted in pain and clutched a bloodied hand to his chest. Grimm advanced and stood over him, one hand holding the gun in readiness, the other knocking burning embers from his own clothing. The guy was going to be no extra threat; looked as though he'd got a chunk missing from his hand.

'You'll live,' the Reaper grunted.

Lenny began to groan and Grimm looked across the clearing. The young man was coming to, rubbing the back of his skull. 'Jeez, what happened?' he spluttered.

Grimm chuckled. 'The cavalry came in the nick of time.'

'Cavalry?' the man queried, looking around incredulously. 'Don't see no cavalry.'

'Don't be stupid, you dumb cluck,' the older one grunted through clenched teeth as he gripped his wrist tight in an attempt to block the pain.

'Never mind, Lenny,' Grimm said patronizingly. 'Just get on your feet and come over here. Get on the ground by your boss where I can keep an eye on the pair of you.' The young man complied, still holding his head.

Keeping the men covered Grimm shucked the cartridges from their weapons and dropped the pistols in the centre of the fire. Then, laying down his own pistol where he could easily pick it up, he untied the rope from around his ankle. He found out his own gunbelt and buckled it in place.

He had to work quick. He could get the hell out, no problem. He had unfinished business in Yellowrock. But these bozos were intent on getting Whitworth's wagon and it wouldn't be long before their compadres returned to learn of his escape and headed out. There was every chance they would fetch up at the Stanhopes. That would put Sarah in jeopardy again. Jeez, that girl; would he never be rid of thinking of her welfare?

No avoiding it – he had to get back to that goddamn shack, and quick. There was a strong chance the other three had heard the explosions and would be on their way back even now. He'd been lucky to down two men the way he had but taking on another three, men whom this time would be prepared, and in the darkness, would be calling on the services of Lady Luck a mite too much. Even if the hardcases hadn't heard the explosions they'd be back by sun-up and would be on his trail for sure.

In the dark there wasn't much to choose between the horses. He selected one and scatted the other two. Without a word he rode into the darkness.

SEVENTEEN

Some distance on and unable to chart a true course in the dark, Grimm was forced to rein in. He took the opportunity to rest up and attempt some sleep, but he had no blanket roll and his mind was needled by thoughts of Sarah's safety. As a consequence his sleep was fitful and, dampened by dew and with the dull ache of tension in his temple, he roused at the first sign of light. He saddled the sorrel and pushed on. The day was well established when he made the Stanhopes' place.

From her vantage point on the verandah where she had been dressing a rough-hewn doll, Sarah was the first to see him. By the time he drew in she was at the hitchrail ready to take his reins. The homesteader put down the scythe he had been sharpening on a grindstone in front of the shack. 'It's Mr Grimm, Hetty,' he shouted. 'Get the coffee on.'

'Hi, Sarah,' Grimm said as he dismounted. She took the reins from him and looped them around the rail without replying or looking at him. He tousled her hair and exchanged greetings with the Stanhopes.

'How's Holser?' he asked, taking off his hat and

rubbing his aching temple.

'Recovering,' the man said. 'The missus's been looking after him. He's sleeping at the moment. He should be able to ride soon.'

The woman returned indoors to prepare the coffee and Sarah went back to the verandah to attend to the needs of her doll.

Grimm gestured for Stanhope to follow him and he leant on the hitchrail. 'Those road agents the lawman talked of,' he said when he had ensured that the females were out of earshot, 'I ran into them. I managed to get away but they're after the wagon.'

'What happened?'

Grimm related the story, concluding with, 'The upshot is I've kinda disrupted their operation, but that don't mean we shouldn't expect them here. They're mean hombres. If they come, there'll be at least three. Mebbe five.'

He looked back whence he had journeyed. 'I been putting my mind to how best we can handle this. They gotta be distracted. I don't want them near this place if I can help it. Help me harness up the mules.' He pointed along his backtrail to a rise on the skyline. 'That knoll yonder. We'll get the wagon up there and leave it on the top where they can see it if they come. It's the load that they're after. Mebbe if we leave it for them they'll be content with that.' The last sentence was spoken without conviction. 'But we can't bet on it. After what I done they'll be after me too.' He replaced his hat. 'So I aim to ride on. I'll take Sarah.'

He rubbed his whiskered chin. 'I told 'em I'd abandoned the wagon after a wheel had broke. When we get it up there we could break the wheel to make it consistent with the story. On the other hand, leaving it intact gives them the chance to drive it away and be out of your hair. It's worth trying.'

When they got back from putting the wagon in place the injured lawman was leaning against the door jamb. 'Why've you left the wagon out there?' he asked.

'Ran into your road agents,' Grimm said. 'I messed up a couple of 'em getting away. I'm riding out with the girl. There's a chance the bushwhackers will be heading out this way so we've left them the wagon.'

Holser absorbed the news. 'You'll be slowed down with the girl and, if they light out after you, they'll catch you easy. What's more, the wagon being where it is, I figure they'll guess Stanhope here had a hand in helping you. They're mean cusses and might seek to take revenge on him and his property.'

The bounty-hunter had thought of that and nodded.

'Reckon it's best you stay here till the threat's over,' the lawman went on. 'If they come a-calling, three against five is better than two.'

Grimm nodded again and voiced his decision. 'I'll go along with that.' He looked at the man's head. 'Anyways, how are you? Got over that bump I gave you?'

Tenderly the lawman felt his head, then shrugged. 'I've had harder knocks.' He looked at Stanhope. 'More important, you got guns and ammo?'

'Enough.'

'OK,' the lawman said. 'We won't tell your missus

or the girl. What they don't know they can't fret about.'

It was an hour later. Grimm was assembling his forty-fours, having soaked their components in oil for a spell. With their weapons primed, the other two men were keeping watch at windows while Sarah and the woman were out of the way in a back room.

'There,' Holser suddenly said. 'Riders.'

Grimm squinted, his eyes not as perceptive as the younger man's. He could just make out movement. 'How many?'

'Five.'

'Five,' Grimm echoed. 'So the two injured bozos I told you about are fit enough to ride,' he concluded, completing the assembly of his guns and moving to the window. Then, as the riders topped the hill, he could see them better as they silhouetted against the blue sky. They halted at the wagon and a couple dismounted to investigate. Minutes passed as the contents were checked.

'They're looking this way,' Holser said. There was a pause, then, 'Now they're heading down.'

Slowly the bunch began to descend the grade. 'I'll go out,' Stanhope said. 'See if I can halt 'em. Tell 'em we don't welcome visitors.'

'That's one opening hand,' Holser said. 'But it's your neck and I didn't want to suggest it. We don't want 'em knowing Grimm is here if it can be avoided. If that's what you're gonna do, Mr Stanhope, you've got to challenge them before they come within gun range. We don't want them close. There's no telling what renegades like that are capable of. Mebbe they'll go. If they don't, you'll have time to get back to the safety of the house.'

'We'll cover you,' Grimm said as Stanhope moved away from the window. The homesteader opened the door and crossed the verandah. Some yards away from the building, he halted and fired his rifle skywards. The five advancing riders reined in.

'Don't come no further,' Stanhope yelled. 'State your business.'

The two men back in the shack could just make out the responding voice on the wind. 'We're after the driver of the wagon back there,' one of the men called. 'Calls himself Morgan. You send him out and there won't be no trouble, mister.'

'Ain't nobody here of that name,' Stanhope replied.

'Then you won't mind us coming down to have a look-see.' The riders began to move but Stanhope's gun, fired skyward, halted them again.

'I'm a law-abiding settler,' he shouted, 'and we keeps ourselves to ourselves. Don't want no truck with strangers. So carry on your way.'

There was a pause as though the men were talking amongst themselves but it became clear riding away was not part of their intent.

Grimm slipped unseen from the door and crouch-walked across the verandah to drop behind a barrel within talking distance of Stanhope. 'There's gonna be more trouble here than we can handle,' he said to the homesteader. He was having second thoughts about involving the settler. 'Stall 'em as long as you can. I'll fix up a horse and make sure they see me head out. That'll draw 'em away from your place.'

'No,' Stanhope said in a low voice. 'You stay put. We're in this thing together.'

'Listen, you don't owe me nothing,' Grimm said. 'You don't even know me.'

'True. I don't know much about you. I don't even know what your real business is. It ain't wagon-driving, that's for sure. But I know one thing, fella. You're a good man. I've seen it in the little girl's eyes, what she thinks of you. You and her's taking my hospitality and that's the way it is. Now get back in the house.'

As he finished the riders began to advance, loosing off rifle shots as they did so. Stanhope backed off and made it inside with Grimm following and closing the door.

'Grimm wants to lead 'em away,' the homesteader said to Holser.

'Won't work,' the lawman said, dropping the wooden bar across the door. 'Get yourselves back to the windows. We're gonna have to make a stand.'

EIGHTEEN

The three men readied their weapons and took up position but immediately flattened themselves adjacent to their respective windows as bullets struck the outer wall. Grimm's fingers worked the catch free. Tilting the frame, he dropped to one knee and fired over the lower edge.

'They've scattered!' Stanhope shouted after he'd thrown his own first volley.

Two-way gunfire resounded, glass shattered, metal dug deep into adobe, then there was quiet for a spell. Grimm held back, proning himself against the wall at the side of the window. He could hear Dwight shouting instructions to his men. The bounty-hunter triggered a couple of shots through the gap but a volley of bullets racketing through the voided frame of the window forced him to duck back out of the line of fire once more.

Quiet again for many minutes. The defenders reloaded and threw questioning glances at each other. It was foolhardy to chance a look through the windows. Then Grimm caught the sound of a disturbed horse snuffling in the corral. The bastards were moving in. He swivelled his face away from the window as a remaining shard of glass shattered and a bullet embedded itself in the far wall. 'Take a back window,' he told Holser. But, even as he spoke, the rise in the volume of gunfire and its source made it plain the occupants were surrounded.

For a moment there was another lull then Dwight's voice could be heard. 'You're surrounded and there's nothing stopping us razing this place to the ground. We know you're in there, Morgan – or whatever your name is. Throw out your guns and come out with your hands up. Save these poor folks from a hard time they don't deserve.'

Holser came to the connecting door. 'The barn's burning.' Grimm caught the look on Stanhope's face; the look of a man experiencing years of work going up in smoke. But the homesteader said nothing. It was up to Grimm.

There was no way the three men could handle this. And it was too late for him to make a break for it and draw them off like he'd said. There was one thing: he could give himself up. There was a slim chance the renegades would be satisfied with that. 'I'm going out to them,' Grimm said, sheathing his guns.

'You know that's crazy,' Stanhope said. He had to raise his voice to continue as spasmodic gunfire resumed, clearly intended as a reminder of their predicament. 'Don't listen to him,' he went on. 'You won't be doing us no favour. Those roustabouts will cause us whatever trouble they choose after they've gunned you down.'

Grimm didn't continue the debate. There was Sarah and the woman to think of. The time for contemplating and talking was over. Narrowing his eyes, Grimm opened the door before either of the two other men could do anything, and stepped outside.

'This is Morgan,' he shouted. 'I'm coming out. I'm doing it in the understanding you'll leave these folks alone.'

He waited for a moment then cautiously moved forward, hands raised. As he did so the hammer of gunfire relented.

'Well, I'll be!' He recognized Dwight's voice. 'The bozo's seeing sense. Come on, Morgan. Drop your guns and walk well clear of the shack. Mark me, if this is some trick we'll burn the whole of this place to the ground.'

Grimm had no tricks, no thoughts on how he could escape the situation. This was something he was walking straight into, eyes open. He shucked his guns and raised his hands again. He moved forward and passed the water trough. Then, past the chicken run and on to the rough trail that led away from the shack. From the corners of his eyes he sensed figures shadowing him at some distance. 'That's far enough,' he heard.

He halted. 'You two,' the boss shouted to some underlings, 'cover the house.'

Then two men were at Grimm's side and Dwight appeared before him, his right hand swathed in a dirty, bloody wrapping. 'You damn mule driver,' he snarled, raising his bandaged appendage. 'You're gonna regret you ever did this.'

'You're gonna leave the settlers be?' Grimm said. 'That's why I've walked out like this.'

'We'll see. I'm calling the shots now. Casey, gimme your gun.'

A man at Grimm's side spun his Remington so that it was butt-first to his boss. Dwight took it awkwardly in his left hand. 'Now hold him fast.'

Strong hands suddenly gripped the Reaper's arms.

'Now hold out one of his hands.'

'Which one, boss?'

'Don't matter. I'm gonna blast both of 'em.' Devilish satisfaction was already apparent in Dwight's grimy face. 'Don't worry, mister,' he leered. 'I ain't gonna kill yuh. You just ain't gonna tote no gun again is all.' He chuckled. 'You's even gonna have trouble wielding a set of wagon reins.'

Grimm's right hand was pushed forward in a vice-grip. At the sight of the advancing barrel he clenched his fist, instinctively in the same manner with which one tenses in a sudden fall. But the best way to fall is to relax, then you roll, minimizing injury. That's why a drunk rarely hurts himself. He hasn't got the reflexes to tense himself. For that reason, Grimm opened his hand, exposing the palm, an action difficult to accomplish in the face of the black maw of the closing gun, standard .45 calibre and looking like a cavern. Hand opened out, he figured at least that way he might save his fingers. Either way, fingers or palms, his bounty-hunting days were over, that was for sure.

The boss worked back the hammer and pushed the muzzle hard in to the centre of Grimm's hand.

Bang!

NINETEEN

The fat man's body whipped sidewise as though someone had whopped him on the shoulder with a hefty length of lumber. Grimm felt his arms released as his captors went for their guns and made for cover. Certain only of his sudden and unexpected freedom, he scrambled back towards the shack as bullets whined. He scooped up his discarded pistols and dived behind the water trough.

He came up in a defensive posture, his guns ready. Casey was behind a rock, nursing a bloodied arm. Dwight was prone with a shoulder wound. The other three had their guns out but weren't firing. Their hesitancy told of puzzlement at suddenly being fired upon from unexpected directions.

There was a lull in the shooting and a voice shouted, 'This is the marshal of Lobo Wells. Drop your weapons if you know what's good for you.' There was a pause, then three pairs of hands complied and rose into the air.

One by one figures emerged from cover, making a total of four lawmen. Holser and Stanhope suddenly appeared at Grimm's side. The bounty-hunter got to his feet and the three men moved forward to complete the circle around the renegades.

'You OK, Clay?' the marshal shouted after he had got the gang leader to his feet.

'Yeah, Marshal. You sure-as-hell turned up in the nick of time.'

'I'll endorse that, Marshal,' Grimm said. He stepped forward towards the lawman and put out his hand. 'Let me shake you by the hand I nearly didn't have.'

'Get the cuffs on the varmints,' the marshal instructed his men before he took the extended hand. Then, 'Glad to be of service,' he said to the bounty-hunter. He turned to his comrade. 'What in tarnation happened to you, Clay?' he asked. 'We couldn't find hide nor hair of yuh.'

'A little misunderstanding along the trail.' The deputy threw a glance at Grimm then looked back at his boss. 'It ain't important. I'll tell yuh about it later.'

'Well, we wus looking for you when we heard the ruckus over here,' the marshal went on. 'We rode over in the direction of the shots, is all. It had quieted when we got in sight but we could see there was some kind of funny business going on. We didn't tally these bozos but then we recognized the wagon-driver. Saw they wus about to blast his hand. So we put an oar in.'

Mrs Stanhope supplied coffee and over steaming mugs, stories were exchanged. Grimm's experiences of the previous night confirmed that the gang were the road agents after the wagon.

'I'll carry on taking the wagon to Yellowrock,' Grimm suggested. 'If that's OK with you, Marshal?'

It would still be good cover for him although he didn't reveal his true intention.

'Yeah,' the marshal said. 'That's OK. The supplies have still got to be delivered one way or another. You shouldn't meet any more trouble now the gang's in custody. When I get back to town I'll mention the part you've played in their apprehension. I figure Whitworth is likely to show his appreciation with a bonus.'

The lawman looked at Sarah sitting with her legs hanging over the edge of the verandah. 'I'll take the girl back. Should be able to find someone in town who'll take her.'

'I ain't going to no town,' Sarah said without looking up. 'Ain't going to live with no strangers. I'm staying with my uncle.'

The marshal looked at Grimm and the bounty-hunter shrugged in silent acquiescence. Sometimes you don't argue. If she insisted on tagging along he'd just have to make sure she was out of the way when he faced up to Von Hoffman.

The marshal and his men got the renegades mounted up and then they headed out.

Half an hour later, it was time to go. Fed and watered, the mules were back in harness. Grimm saw that Sarah was once more up in the driver's seat and then went inside the building to say his goodbyes to Mrs Stanhope.

'Thank you kindly for your hospitality, ma'am,' he said. 'And I'm real sorry I brought you and your husband so much trouble. But it all worked out.'

Inexplicably, tears welled up in the woman's eyes and she sought refuge in a back room without speaking. Perplexed Grimm stood alone for a moment, then went outside.

'Your lady seems unwell,' he said to Stanhope. 'She ain't sickening with something, is she?'

The man shook his head and averted his eyes without comment.

Grimm cast a quartering eye around the terrain. The departing riders were long out of sight by this time and there was nothing to the horizon. 'It sure must be hard on a woman out here,' he added.

Stanhope looked at him, still without speaking, then said, 'No, there's more to it than that. Let me show you something before you go.'

He led the bounty-hunter round the back of the shack and past the outbuildings. There was a small rise well beyond the animal pens and vegetable patch. They walked silently to the top where Stanhope halted before a small cross marking a low mound of earth. 'Our son, Mr Grimm. Danny. Nine years old.'

Grimm took off his hat.

'Went down with some ailment or other,' Stanhope went on, biting his lip to hold back the emotion in his voice. 'You know, the way kids do. Anyways, within a day he had died. Just like that. It happened so quick.' There were tears in his eyes now. 'As it fell,' he sighed, 'we'd just buried him the day you arrived.'

The information sent a whoosh of emotion through the listener. 'Jeez, I'm sorry, Mr Stanhope. I didn't know.'

'You had no way of knowing. There was no point in telling you. It was our private sorrow and you had your own troubles.'

Grimm nodded almost imperceptibly. What the man said explained a lot: the black clothes Grimm had noticed on that first day, their drawn faces and unhappy demeanour. Then there had been Mrs Stanhope's constant retiring to her room. He thinking she was ill. It all fitted now.

'What a day for me to turn up,' Grimm said in a low voice. 'I should have guessed something like that. Where angels fear to tread, fools rush in. I don't know what to say. What you gonna do now?'

'Pick up the pieces. If we can't, if the place holds too many memories, we'll move out I reckon.'

The two men walked in silence down the hill. Back at the wagon Grimm shook Stanhope's hand before putting on his gloves and hauling himself up into the driving seat alongside Sarah. 'Pass my condolences to your good lady.'

Stanhope nodded and with that Grimm flicked the reins and the wagon began to roll.

TWENTY

The place was just like other sites he had known where men dug raw gold out of the earth. The assay office, housed in a wooden shack, was the only construction that looked as though it might not blow away at the first wind. The other places of business that he could see as he nudged the wagon into camp had been more hastily constructed. A saloon to his right was a lean-to with nothing to lean to. An equipment store on his left consisted of logs with nothing more than loose planking for a roof. Other facilities were even less permanent: beer tents, wagons serving as supply depots. Outside the blacksmith's tent, the smith noisily worked some metal over an anvil. Away from the muddy central thoroughfare a whole town of assorted tents and coverings housed the miners.

Here and there: open corrals with ponies and burros. A black-clothed preacher made his points with upraised hand and intense eyes that alone could have nailed a sinner to the cross that stood behind him. A one-eyed beggar stuck out a grasping palm. They were all here: the good, the bad, the ugly.

Ahead of the lead mules, dust-covered men

crossed the track. The day's light was beginning to fail and workers were leaving their diggings. Men were coming out of the ground, panners were leaving the streams. There were few with any look of hope in their eyes. Grimm wondered how many were pulling something that would at least earn their keep? How many were already working a worthless claim? And how long it would be before this too was a ghost camp, like the rest of them.

He passed a vast woodlot where men were working timber into manageable shapes; with winter approaching, probably the most profitable business in town. Further on, he halted the mules alongside a man sitting on an upturned keg outside the barber's tent having his head shaved. For those miners who worked underground a head of matted hair could be a flea-infested liability.

'Supply wagon from Lobo Wells,' Grimm said. 'Where can I find Jess Henderson? I'm told he takes delivery.'

The nearly-bald man sprang into unexpected life, grabbed the barber's cloth from around his neck and wiped the lumpy remnants of lather from his head. 'You from Whitworth?'

'Yeah.'

'Then you got baccy aboard.' There was expectancy in the voice.

'Reckon so.'

'Jehosophat!' the man exclaimed, standing up and shoving a coin into the barber's hand. 'Will the boys be glad to see you. There's a tobacco famine in camp. Ain't had a good chew myself for a week. The stuff's almost the price of gold dust.' He stepped animatedly off the boards into the mud. 'Follow me, pardner.' He took the bridle of the lead mules. 'That shack twenty yards up, that's Jess's place of business.'

'Obliged,' Grimm said, flicking the reins as the old prospector began to tug the animals along the rutted thoroughfare.

The supply shack was a ramshackle frame building that had the look of a construction that had served its best years elsewhere only to have been dismantled and set up here for a new lease of life.

'You Jess Henderson?' Grimm asked the guy waiting outside to greet the arrival of his stocks.

'Yeah,' he shouted up to Grimm as he took the bridle of the lead mules from the old-timer. 'Expected you a day ago. Had trouble?'

Grimm hauled on the brake. 'Yeah. Gang of road agents.'

'What happened? They been playing damned havoc with the run.'

'Well, it's all over now. Marshal's taking 'em into Lobo Wells.' He helped Sarah down. 'I'll give you the details when I got a cup of coffee in front of me.'

It was some time later and they were finishing coffee in the room that served as the supply office. 'I've got a cot you're welcome to use for the night,' Henderson said. He looked at the girl. 'Your gal?'

Grimm nodded.

'Figure we can fix up the little lady too,' Henderson offered.

Sarah continued smoothing the blue dress of her doll and said nothing.

'Listen,' Grimm said, taking the pipe from his mouth and wiping moisture from his lips, 'you'll know most of the men in camp, won't yuh, Jess?'

'Sure. In this line, everybody comes a-calling sometime.'

'You know of a guy called Von Hoffman shacking up here?'

'No, can't say as I do.'

Grimm nodded. 'He might be operating under a different name. You know how it is.'

'Friend of yours?'

'Yeah,' Grimm said with a chuckle. He tried to remember the features on the reward dodger and the description they'd given him back in Fort Smith. 'Tall, square-faced, slight limp in the right leg.'

It was Henderson's turn to smile. 'That description would fit a helluva lotta guys round here. A sizeable proportion are limping or got crook arms or summat.'

Grimm chuckled to cover his annoyance. 'Yeah, reckon it would.'

It was some time later. Sarah had been so tired she could hardly open her mouth to eat the grub that Henderson had rustled up, so Grimm had got her bedded down, then gone for a mosey around the camp. He had a problem. The features on reward posters weren't reliable at the best of times but at least they were a guide. Without even that he hadn't got a foot in the stirrup.

He glanced inside a couple of the tents that served as saloons then decided on the main beer tent. At least it was less cramped but, like the others, it was dingy, smoky and noisy. The canvas roof sagged in the middle and, although there was actually clearance for a man of his height, he instinctively ducked his head as he moved around. He took a drink and sat at one of the beer kegs that did duty as a table. Henderson was right. The description he had given him of Von Hoffman could fit almost any of them. Some kind of injury, a limp or a scar, went with the job working under ground.

He listened to men describing their day. Watched the comings and goings. Observed the money-lenders extending meagre credit to unfortunates locked in a cycle of work and debt.

He saw an old man enter and stand in the doorway. He wore scruffy threadbare clothes but, unlike the others, he didn't bear the soil marks of labour. The curves of a frown marked his features and his lower jaw jutted out determinedly, like an undershot bulldog. He stabbed the air with a penetrating stare as he surveyed the occupants. His appraisal concluded when his eyes fell on a young man leaning on the bar.

He stomped over and presented himself alongside the drinker. 'That's my claim you're working, you varmint.'

The younger man turned and took stock of the speaker. 'We been working it a week. How come you only just shooting your mouth off?'

"Cos I been flat on muh back with ague, that's why.'

The younger man looked away and disinterestedly took a slug of his drink. 'Get back in your wheelchair, you old panhandler.'

The old man grabbed his arm. 'I want you offa muh claim, you hear, you roustabout?'

In one movement the young man whirled round and smashed his mug down on the speaker's forehead. The oldster collapsed to lie crumpled on the boards, inert and covered in beer dregs.

Grimm didn't like to see that, but the damage was done; and it wasn't his affair. Just thought, here we go again. There was a lull as the young man ordered the bartender to fill up his mug, then conversations resumed around the room. Grimm spied an onlooker by the door slip out, unseen by the hardcase at the counter.

'Somebody get that stiff outa the way,' the young man said after he'd taken another drink. 'Damned critter's causing an obstruction.'

A couple of spectators emerged from the crowd and began to drag the still form of the oldster towards the door. As they got to the entrance a new face appeared. There was a no-nonsense look in the eyes, a gun in hand. The man stepped aside as the miner's form was manoeuvered past the door. The man who had slipped out earlier was by his side. He pointed and the newcomer took his cue. 'You,' he said, advancing on the one who had dropped the old man, 'come with me.'

The young man looked at the newcomer and his gun with some surprise. 'What the hell you talking about?'

'Claim-jumping is a matter for Benson to work out,' the new arrival said, his voice matter-of-fact.

'Who's Benson?'

'You'll find out. Gimme your irons and let's git moving.'

'There ain't no law to answer to here,' the young man retorted without moving.

'That's what you think, son,' the other said, slowly resuming his advance. 'Now come along easy-like 'cos I'm sure losing my patience.'

Unseen by the 'lawman', a man close to Grimm drew his gun and levelled it at the speaker. Yeah, here we go again, Grimm thought. Up till now he hadn't interfered but he didn't like to see someone get jumped for trying to keep the peace. So he cut in and a split second later the muzzle of Grimm's gun was touching the man's temple. 'No, you don't,' the bounty-hunter muttered. 'Drop it. Fair's fair.'

The gun clattered to the boards. The lawman kept his gun trained on the first man and threw a glance at the second and the discarded gun. 'You can come in too,' he said. 'You got some explaining to do.' As he took the offered gun from the man at the bar he was joined by a fellow officer who had pushed his way in. The two began to shepherd the trouble-makers out. 'Obliged, mister,' the first 'lawman' said to Grimm as he passed him on his way out.

Grimm just nodded and returned to his drink. Helping out in bar-room brawls was becoming a habit. Again, conversations broke out and the scene was as though nothing had happened. It was some time later that a man came and sat at Grimm's table. He looked more like a camp-follower than a miner or panner. 'I've seen you before,' he said in a loud liquor-laden voice. 'You're a bounty, ain't yuh?'

The statement was made loud enough to catch the ears of those nearby and its content of the nature to hook their interest. 'Paid it no mind till you drew that gun of yours,' he went on. 'I was across the room at the time and just happened to be looking at you. I never seed your hand move it was that fast. Like greased lightning. One second you was still, next you had a shooter pointing at that guy's head. Only a regular gunny has that kinda speed. I thought I'd seed you afore. Set me thinking. Then it came to me. Years aback, out in Arizona. Taking in a renegade to the marshal's office in Prescott. A bounty-hunter. The one they call The Reaper.'

'Not me, fella,' Grimm said, shaking his head.

'That was you, boy,' the man went on. His fingers explored a different part of his face each time he spoke: stroking his cheek, probing his nostrils, feeling his lips. 'Yeah, sure as day is day.' He nodded at the listeners in satisfaction, then stood up and wandered away in a drunken stupor.

Grimm had denied the drunk's claim but the damage was done. His cover was blown. Every coyhoot for miles would know a bounty-hunter was in town.

TWENTY-ONE

He drew on his pipe as he pondered on his next move. Yeah, news that a bounty-hunter was in camp would spread like a prairie fire in the dry season. And folk would figure there could only be one reason why a bounty-hunter had ridden out to a God-forsaken hole like Yellowrock: he would have his sights on some no-good with his face on a dodger. Hell, his cards were exposed now and there was nothing for it but to play the hand, open as it was for all at the table to see. One advantage: he could openly ask questions now. It didn't matter now who knew his business.

Who would be good for information? Yeah, there would be one man in the camp who would know if there was a renegade like Von Hoffman around. A man who made it his business to know everything. Seems like in Yellowrock it could be a guy called Benson.

'Who's Benson?' he asked the old-timer seated near him.

'You must be new in town, stranger,' the old man said. 'Big Jake Benson is what goes for law around here.'

'Law?' his partner echoed. 'He's everything!'

'Where can I find him?'

'Ain't no secret. North end of camp. Log cabin, big place. A blind raccoon couldn't miss it.'

Grimm dropped a dollar on the table, nodded a thanks and stepped outside.

In the context of the scatteration of dilapidated constructions that made up Yellowrock, Benson's place was impressive, solid log with frame addition, impervious to the elements. He knocked on the door and was admitted by one of the men he had seen dispensing justice in the saloon.

Inside, the place was well-furnished, incongruous in Yellowrock, like he'd stepped into another world. A man sat at a table with glass and a bottle of top dollar whiskey. His tailored suit too looked out of place in a mining camp, as did the expensive patterned boots.

'Jake Benson?' Grimm asked.

'Benson,' the dude confirmed. 'Wondered how long it'd be afore you came a-calling. Pleased to make your acquaintance, Mr Grimm.'

'How d'you know my name?'

'Word came to me there was a bounty-hunter in camp. Only one bounty I know of fits the description given to me.' He took another glass from a side-table, picked up the bottle and, as the neck hovered over the glass, he looked at Grimm for acceptance of the offer.

Grimm nodded.

'From Arizona to Kansas, so I hear,' the dude continued as he began to pour. 'And there seems to be more to the killing of Jesse James than was in the papers. Am I warm?'

'I really don't know what you're talking about.'

'I can understand the reticence,' Benson

rejoined as he filled the glass. 'Well, we won't go into that. Let's just say I got admiration for the man who pulled it and made it look like the way it was*. Did law-abiding folks a good turn. Talking of good turns, Huckabee, my man here, tells me you did him a good turn tonight.'

'That's right, boss,' Huckabee said. 'Stopped one of them buckaroos getting the jump on me with his gun.'

Grimm stepped forward and took the glass. 'Don't cotton to seeing a gun pulled behind a man's back is all.'

'Nevertheless, we're obliged. Your health, Mr Grimm.'

Grimm acknowledged the toast and downed his drink. 'They tell me you're the big honcho in Yellowrock.'

Benson grunted in cynical satisfaction. 'Is that what they say?'

Grimm was familiar with the scenario. A tough camp like this, far from the grasp of official legal bodies, would generate its own law enforcement apparatus. In the beginning there would be beat-ups, claim-jumping and killings. There was always someone who would step forward and offer protection services. He and his boys could be genuine or they could be responsible for much of the trouble themselves. From that could develop a law enforcement system of sorts that would start to grow under its own momentum. Part of the process would be the early insistence that all miners pay the subscription. Miners would go for this, not only

* Readers wishing to understand this part of the conversation should refer to 'Dollars for the Reaper' (Hale, 1990)

because it would cut down freeloaders but it would act as an obstacle for newcomers. But the assumption of arbitrary power carries the seeds of corruption. However, it would have to do until proper law moved up from the towns. That is, if the lode lasted long enough.

Such a set-up always threw up somebody who would be top of the heap. It had taken only one enquiry to reveal that, in Yellowrock, it was Big Jake Benson.

'We're two of a kind,' Benson went on. 'You and me. We fill in the cracks the law leaves. Anyways, I'm sure this ain't a social call. What can I do for you?'

'I'm looking for a renegade. Name of Von Hoffman. The last I heard seemed he was holing up here.'

'You got a dodger?'

Grimm shook his head. 'Lost it a ways back. Can't remember the critter's face too well either. Medium build, square face.'

Benson looked unimpressed.

'Figure with a name like that,' Grimm went on, 'he might have an accent. Dutch, German, something like that.'

'I think I know your man,' Huckabee said. 'There's a bozo with a funny accent camped up on the slope with another couple of guys.'

'Yeah,' Benson added. 'I know the ones. Thought there was something fishy, 'cos it's plain they ain't no miners. The only times we see 'em in Yellowrock is when they use one of the saloons.'

'Keep disappearing too,' Huckabee went on. 'Scuttle-butt is they had a fracas with some fella out on the trail and shot him. Only rumours, though.'

Grimm nodded. 'That'd be another bounty chaser. Came across him recovering from a dose of lead in Lobo Wells. They musta thought they'd finished him.'

Benson shrugged. 'But, like Huckabee says, it's only scuttle-butt. This foreigner's a man of uncertain temperament but knows when to draw his horns in. They ain't caused no trouble in camp so I got no beef with him or his sidekicks.'

'Figures,' Grimm said, getting to his feet. 'If they were holing up here for a spell, they'd aim to keep out of trouble. Well, if you'll excuse me, I figure I'll look them up.'

Benson looked serious. 'Doing Huckabee a good turn, you did yourself one. Otherwise we'd be taking half the bounty.' Then his features eased. 'But seeing's you helped us out we'll forget it. Like I said, you and me's two of a kind. Any way I can help you, let me know.'

Grimm moved to the door. 'Obliged for the drink, Mr Benson.'

'Hope you catch the critter,' Benson said in a raised voice as he made his exit. 'You watch yourself. Like as not, they'll know you're after 'em by now.'

Why he went first to the supplies building, he didn't know. When he got there it was quiet. 'Henderson,' he called as he closed the door. There was no answer. He thought maybe the fellow had gone out for a drink but then he heard groaning. He found the man lying on the wooden planking.

'What happened?' Grimm asked, stooping down and helping the fellow into a sitting position.

'Two bozos bust in,' the man grunted. 'Afore I could do anything one of 'em had cracked me on the head.'

Grimm let the man go, grabbed a lantern and dashed into the back room. He felt a chill go up his spine. Sarah's cot was empty.

TWENTY-TWO

Grimm made his way back to Benson's. 'That offer of help,' he said when once more inside, 'you mean it?'

'Of course,' the man said. 'How can I be of service?'

Grimm explained what had happened. 'So I'm in need of a couple of damn good horses,' he concluded. 'I'm sure it's Von Hoffman now. Taking the girl like this is as good as admitting it. The bastard's using her as a hostage.'

'Afraid I can't spare any men. It might be a long trek and I need both of my men to hold down trouble here. Diggings are getting poorer and tempers are fraying around the camp.'

'Makes no odds. I always work alone. Something good to ride is all I need.'

'We got some top-dollar stock out back. Huckabee will help you pick a good pair.'

When Grimm returned, an old-timer was hobbling out through the door.

'Your men are making it up into the foothills,' Benson said. 'Two. That oldster saw 'em. Going at a helluva lick so he came to tell me about it.'

'Is there much that happens in the camp that you don't know?'

'What I don't know ain't worth knowing.' Benson stood up, took a map from a drawer and unfurled it on a table. It was an amateur job marked out on thick paper. 'See, there's a scratchy trail up across the foothills.' He indicated it with his forefinger. 'Not used much now the mine's played out. There's the mine. No point in setting out until there's light. You won't make it in the dark. It's only a track. Have another drink.'

At daybreak Grimm could feel the freshness of the wind coming down the slopes. On one of Benson's prime horses and with a clutch of dynamite from the store in his saddle-bag, he splashed over the shallow stream at the end of the camp and kept to the track which followed the stream up into the foothills. Then, some distance on, the trail left the stream to cut through the pines.

Till now Von Hoffman had just meant dollar signs to the bounty-hunter. Grimm hadn't cared how he brought him to book just as long as he'd got him in tow. Then the owlhoot had taken Sarah for leverage. That had been a mistake. Now Grimm's frame of mind was more than disinterested.

With his saddle on a fresh mount and a relief horse in tow, Grimm made good headway, satisfied in the knowledge that Von Hoffman and his sidekicks would be moving at a slower pace on account of having taken Sarah. Even though they'd left some hours before him they had had the blackness of night with which to contend. There was only one trail up into the hills and he could follow that without any trouble. All he had to do was keep his eyes skinned in case they had some idea about jumping him.

At a higher elevation the wind became keener and the trail became rougher as he progressed further into the hills. In broken country pursuit would be more difficult. He saw no sign of passage and all his bets were on them sticking to the trail. Then he saw horse droppings; fresh droppings.

An hour on, something blue in the thicket caught his attention. He dismounted to examine it. A doll's dress. Sarah was OK and knew he would be following. She had left it as a sign. The cunning little tyke.

It was noon when he sighted the mine that Benson had pointed out on the map. He dismounted and tethered the horses so that he could advance on foot. When he reached the clearing he stayed in the cover of the trees. There were a couple of dilapidated buildings but he couldn't see any horses: just, here and there, the trash left by long-gone workmen. Then, in plain view: a wooden doll in the dust. That gal was a gem. So they were here. OK, then they were probably in the mine itself. Must have taken the horses with them to be out of sight.

He stayed a long spell, just watching. They hadn't arranged for this place to be a hideout so they couldn't stay in there for ever. But neither could he wait for them to show. They probably had enough jerked beef to last the duration.

He looked up at the ragged outline of the mountain beyond. It was an old mine and these things often ran like rabbit warrens through the rock. There might be another means of entry or exit but he didn't have the time to go probing. Anyways, he had to put his bet on the only means of entry being the gaping maw into which the rusting tracks disappeared. Nothing else for it.

He needed something to draw them out; a diversion that would draw their attention, confuse them. He had just the thing; and he still had the advantage of surprise. He gauged the distance from the mine entrance to the nearest shack. He reckoned he could make it. Then he went back to the horses and took out the sticks of dynamite he'd taken from the store.

He circled the open space and worked his way through the foliage above the workings. Little by little he edged his way down towards the entrance, careful where he placed his feet so as not to send down gravel that would draw attention.

He drew his Army Colts, checked them over and returned them to their holsters. He took the clutch of dynamite from the bag and widened his stance, ensuring the ground beneath his feet was firm. He struck a match and applied it to the fuse which crackled into life. He took careful aim and hurled it at the shack. He missed the open door but the bundle hit the ground and bounced to land at the foot of the wall, fizzing against the dry rotted wood. That was good enough.

He covered his ears to mask the explosion but when it came he felt the ground vibrate and the blast of air. He edged a few more feet down, then waited. He didn't have to wait long. From his position he saw a gun-barrel nosing out of the mine below him; then a second gun. They stayed that way for a long time.

All the renegades could see was a dust cloud hovering over a demolished shack. They would be asking themselves questions. The only way they could answer those questions was by coming out to investigate. He could wait.

There were whispered exchanges, then the two

men slowly emerged. One advanced, covering the area before the mine. The other backed out, tracking the grade behind the mine with his gun. His face was vaguely familiar, square-looking; it had to be Von Hoffman.

Grimm stepped from behind the pine. 'Drop your guns!'

The far man turned but Von Hoffman was the first to read the situation and fired. Simultaneously Grimm sidestepped and triggered both his Colts. Von Hoffman was whipped back by the force of the impact as a slug punched his shoulder. The second man made to fire but dropped his gun as a bullet sliced flesh from his forearm, and he fell to his knees muttering an impotent oath.

Grimm loped down and holstered one of his guns so that he could pick up the fallen weapons. As he did so he kept his Colt trained on the injured men but they weren't in a position to cause trouble.

'We still got the girl,' Von Hoffman sneered. 'Now, you drop your guns if you want to see her alive.'

'Where is she?' Grimm snarled.

Suddenly there was a thunderclap behind him, the sound bouncing successively off the cavern walls behind him, prolonging its duration. Recovering from the shattering effect it had on his nervous system he whirled round in a crouch. A figure loomed out of the maw of the mine. Grimm made to fire but the man already had shock writ large in his eyes. A gun dangled uselessly by its trigger-guard from a finger. He took a couple of staggered paces, then dropped to his knees clutching his back.

Grimm moved towards him. 'What the hell …?'

Then he saw Sarah stepping out of the darkness. She held a smoking Navy Colt in two hands. The weapon looked large and awkward in her grip. 'He was going to shoot you,' she said weakly.

Grimm took the gun from her, pushed it into his belt and put his arm around her. 'It's all right, kid. You did fine. Without lessons too.'

Epilogue

With Sarah willingly acting as a nurse, he strapped up the three men's wounds, then got them mounted up and made the slow trek back. At Yellowrock crowds watched as the prisoners were transferred to Whitworth's wagon, then Grimm set out once more for Lobo Wells. There the marshal took the renegades into custody. The lawman had a reward poster on Von Hoffman so identification was no problem and he sent a cable to the federal office notifying them of the outlaw's capture. Receiving authorization he gave the bounty-hunter a chit cashable at a federal office. The owlhoot's sidekicks weren't on a wanted list but the marshal put them in the slammer to face charges of kidnapping on Grimm's written evidence.

With the familiar feel of his Andalusian under his saddle and a couple of relief horses in tow Grimm headed out to take Sarah to her mother. It was the end of the month by the time they rode into Abilene, lather whorls of sweat standing out on the flanks of their horses. The cow-town was new to Grimm but Sarah knew her way about the place and directed him down an alley off Texas Street.

They reined in near some stairs leading to an apartment above a store. He tethered the horses and accompanied the girl up the steps, his feet heavy with tiredness. He knocked at the door which was opened by a woman in her late twenties, rubbing sleep from her eyes.

'What the hell you doing here?' she wanted to know, eschewing any form of greetings.

Sarah turned to descend without speaking but Grimm stayed her. 'Are you Mrs Toomey, ma'am?'

'Yeah, but that kid ain't no responsibility of mine no more.'

'I think we'd better come inside,' Grimm persisted. 'We come a long way and we got things to talk about.'

The conversation didn't last long. The woman clearly had no maternal instincts for the child. Nor was she disturbed that her husband was dead. 'Only got what he deserved,' was her only comment.

She and the outlaw had married young with the child on the way. Plying his trade and always on the run, he hadn't been at home much, leaving the woman mostly to fend for herself with the unwanted child. The undercurrent of her story was that there'd been many men in her life and in such circumstances the child had been a hindrance. She told how, earlier that year, Toomey had turned up again, wanting food and money. This time he had taken the child as well to give himself cover while on the run. The way he figured, a man travelling with a child didn't look suspicious. The mother had had no qualms. It got the kid off her back.

During the conversation the woman's current

man-friend stood silent and unshaven in the background. Grimm listened but knew there was to be no gain in trying to talk about responsibilities to the woman. When he finally realized there was to be no resolution of the situation he felt like telling the woman what he really thought of her. But there was to be no gain from that either. Besides, he didn't feel like letting rip at the mother in Sarah's presence. At least the two travellers got a cup of coffee out of the meeting before they were shown the door. But that was all.

'Son-of-a-bitch,' Sarah said, when they were once more outside the building.

'I thought we had an agreement about cussing,' her aged companion reminded her. 'When all's said and done, she's still your ma.'

The girl ignored his reprimand. 'Told you she didn't want me. Never did.'

Grimm couldn't understand it. He thought mothers were supposed to love their kids. He'd got to know Sarah in the long time they'd been together. She was likeable and becoming a good cook over a camp-fire. And pretty too, on those rare occasions when he had managed to persuade her to get the trail muck offa her face. It pleased him to remember how she looked when she cupped her hands and delicately lapped clear stream water, and how she giggled at the antics of prairie dogs. Jeez, how could such a kid be not wanted? As a bounty-hunter his world was full of bastards. But a woman could be a bastard too.

He looked down the street. Abilene was now an established cow-town and a new herd of longhorns was just being driven in. The breeze brought the choking dust churned up by the hooves billowing down the street. The boardwalks were crowded with hard-bitten punchers and piano music jangled from the saloons. The men were raucous and foul-mouthed. Natural for men after long months in the saddle. But this was no place for a young girl. Yeah, but where *was* her place?

'I got an idea,' he said after a spell of musing. 'But first we'll get out of this dust and get ourselves a bite to eat.'

Weeks later, almost unrecognizable under the trail grime, they reined in at a homestead in the wilderness.

Jim and Hester Stanhope were surprised but glad to see them again. After greetings were exchanged Grimm saw to it that Sarah stayed outside so that he could speak openly to the couple. He related the girl's story how he'd heard it from her mother. He told of his role in killing her outlaw father, the escapades he and the girl had been through together and the responsibility he felt for her. 'So I've made this journey on a long shot,' he concluded. 'You probably figured what I'm a-wondering.'

'You don't have to put it in words, Mr Grimm,' Hester said. She looked across at her husband. 'For my part I'd love to take on the child.'

Her husband nodded. 'It would give meaning to both our lives. Your concerns are at an end, Mr Grimm. That is, if the girl will have us.'

The woman stood up and went outside. Seconds later Sarah came bounding in, joy in her eyes.

So that was that, and Grimm could finally turn his thoughts once more to earning a living. 'I could sure do with another cup of your coffee, ma'am,' he said, relief plain in his voice.

Sarah was soon helping Hester prepare her new bedroom and Grimm relaxed in a chair, chatting with Jim, smoking, browsing through some old magazines. All that was missing was a pair of slippers.

He stayed over a few nights, thankful for the rest, but then it was time to go. He explained to Sarah that he had to leave and go about his business. But he would not forget her and would send her a letter from time to time. After he'd saddled his horse, he took Jim on one side and pulled out a wad of bills. 'There's nearly a thousand bucks there,' he said handing it to the homesteader, 'save for some spending money I've taken.'

'I can't take that, Jonathan.'

'You can and you will,' Grimm insisted. 'With me, big money comes and goes. I'm putting it in your hands as Sarah's guardians. It's yours to do with as you will. What you don't spend in raising the girl, put on one side for when she's older.'

After he'd made his formal goodbyes to the couple they stood on the verandah with Sarah between them. As Grimm made a final check on the cinch the girl broke free from the caring hands, ran forward and came to a standstill in the open space half way between the readied horses and the building, clutching her blue-dressed doll.

Grimm saw her movement and walked back to her. 'You once asked me if I was rich and I said no,' he said, reaching out for her. He put his arms around her and pulled her to him for a moment. He hadn't held someone close like this for a long time. There was an unaccustomed, and uncomfortable, lump in his throat. 'Well, I've changed my mind,' he said, trying to hide his sudden huskiness. 'With you in my life, I'm as wealthy as a king.'

Then he held her at arm's length and looked into her eyes. But he could tell she didn't have much understanding of what he was saying. She was only a kid.

She didn't speak, just backed away a few paces, still clutching the doll. He hauled himself into the saddle and nudged the Andalusian. He turned once, gave a last wave and headed out. Yeah, she was only a kid and wouldn't understand his fanciful speech.

However, that she did bear him similar feelings was indicated by the sad smile that came to her lips as she returned his wave.

But, by then, he was too far away to see.